ISABEL RICARDO

ISBN-13: 978-1-949868-35-7

Copyright © 2021 Isabel Ricardo
Interior Illustrations by Isabel Alves
Cover Illustration by Tiago Silva

Translated by: José Manuel Godinho

Published by Underline Publishing LLC.
www.underlinepublishing.com

All rights reserved.

No part of this publication may be reproduced, distributed or transmitted in any form or by any means, or stored in a database or retrieval system, without the prior written permission of the publisher. The only exception is by a reviewer, who may quote short excerpts in a review.

Published with the support of
DGLAB / Cultura and Camões, IP - Portugal
and the Municipality of Nazaré - Portugal.

Foreword

Dear readers,

This book is the first in a collection that is very popular in Portugal, not only among children, but among teenagers and adults as well. I hope you enjoy reading it as much as I enjoyed writing it.

You will meet Tony and Daniel, Bea and Chris, and, last but not least, the most playful of all the characters: Jack. As you will soon learn, I'm not talking about a child: Jack is a crow—a real one, at that. I can also tell you that my nephews were the inspiration behind the four children.

Let me ask you something: no matter how you wish, never to get into risky situations like our friends do. Caves are dangerous. You must be accompanied by adults. You may fall—even down a hole!—and experience a thousand other unexpected adventures. That is why I wrote this book: so that you could dream of being one of **THE ADVENTURERS** and live this exciting adventure without taking unnecessary risks.

My Grandmother told me the story of the cave where the table and the stone benches could be seen. Many people saw it, too, whenever the sea receded a lot. People used to call it Boca do Inferno, Hell's Mouth.

The cave in which the four cousins entered really exists, except that, sensibly, I did not dare explore it, aware of the risk I would run if I did. The submarine story is also true: the Germans appeared in Nazaré on May 20, 1945—they left no gold, of course. However, fishermen say that sonars beep whenever they sail over the sunken submarine.

The events I tell you about in Chapter 21 took place on August 4 and 5, 1998. Due to climate change, the same thing has happened almost every year ever since.

I wish that *The Adventurers and the Treasure Cave* will be a source of fun and new, enthusiastic fans of **THE ADVENTURERS**, just as it happened with young Portuguese readers.

I would also like to wish a very special thank you to some people: my editor, Nereide Santa Rosa, for her enthusiasm about this collection, helping me fulfil a dream I hold very dear—the publication of **THE ADVENTURERS** in English; Tiago da Silva, for the amazing cover illustration, and Isabel Alves, for the illustrations inside the book; and to the entire team at Underline Publishing, in recognition of their magnificent work.

Love,

Isabel Ricardo

Contents

Chapter 1 - An intriguing phone call 7

Chapter 2 - Bea, Chris... and Jack 15

Chapter 3 - A rather inauspicious beginning 23

Chapter 4 - A very strange attitude 31

Chapter 5 - A very suspicious lodger and a funny prank 39

Chapter 6 - An unpleasant argument 47

Chapter 7 - A very interesting discovery 57

Chapter 8 - Fascinating stories 67

Chapter 9 - Jack has a great time! 77

Chapter 10 - In the chapel 87

Chapter 11 - A different, even more suspicious looking man ... 95

Chapter 12 - At Forte de São Miguel and Forno d'Orca 103

Chapter 13 - The Cave! 113

Chapter 14 - On their way to adventure! 123

Chapter 15 - Deep inside the *suberco* 133

Chapter 16 - Trapped underground! 141

Chapter 17 - Prisoners! 151

Chapter 18 - A big surprise! 159

Chapter 19 - An amazing discovery! 169

Chapter 20 - Hell's Mouth! 177

Chapter 21 - A very happy ending! 189

Chapter 1

An intriguing phone call

The telephone rang annoyingly, startling a woman in her early thirties with black hair and beautiful green eyes.

"Daniel! Be a dear and answer the phone while I put dinner on the table."

A mischievous-looking, tanned eleven-year-old boy ran into the room, mimicking the sound of a motorbike. He reappeared shortly afterwards, pretending to brake suddenly, and sat down at the table.

"It's Godmom! She wants to talk to you. She sounded very mysterious."

His mother put her dish on the counter, annoyed. She didn't like it when people called her on the phone at mealtimes. She headed for the pantry without thinking. When she got there, she stopped, not knowing what she was doing there. She turned as she heard her husband and her children laughing.

"You were going to answer the phone, Mom," Tony said, amused.

She laughed and ran to the living room. She was terribly distracted, which was a source of fun for all the family. She picked up the receiver.

"Hello! It's me. Yeah? I haven't seen him in a while. Of course, the builders are still in your place. No, it's no trouble at all. It'll be great to see the boys again. There are bunk beds in both rooms, so it's fine. You did well. Give me a ring tomorrow. I love you! Give them my love, too."

She hung up and stood there absentmindedly for a moment. Then she went to the kitchen, not even noticing her children's curiosity and her husband's interest. They smiled as they watched her pick up the dishes, which had not been used yet, and take them to the sink.

"If you like washing dishes so much you even wash the ones that are clean, who am I to stop you? We need a couple of those for dinner, though," her husband said, winking at the children. He was a tall, broad-shouldered man, with thick brown hair and dark eyes. He had a very pleasant smile, just like their eldest son.

She laughed and began to serve dinner, oblivious to their curiosity.

"What did Godmom want? Come on!"

"She asked me to do something for her. Cousin Michael called her and asked if his children could stay with her for two weeks. He and his wife have to go away for some time and won't be able to take them along. Of course, my sister agreed. Besides, they had already agreed on it a few months ago. The thing is she hoped that construction work in the new house would be complete by now."

"Then why didn't she say so to Cousin Michael?"

"I'm not sure. To tell you the truth, I didn't understand. Anyway, it doesn't matter. You know my sister and I grew up together with my cousin and his sister. We always felt like brother and sisters to each other, although they were closer to each other despite the age difference. I'd really like to see the children again. I haven't seen them in ages!"

Daniel exchanged a look with his brother and twitched his nose in contempt. "Where will they sleep?"

"In your room, of course. There are two bunk beds. You can sleep in Tony's room."

"Why can't I stay in the empty room?" he asked, annoyed.

"I need it to rent it. Someone may suddenly appear, you know. What's wrong with sleeping in your brother's room? There are bunk beds there, too. What's the difference?"

Daniel was about to open his mouth to reply, but something he saw in his father's gaze stopped him. He was silent for the rest of the meal and ate without appetite. As usual, his brother had no trouble eating, although he was also a little annoyed by the news. It seemed to him that their cousins were possibly a little boring, not to mention snobbish.

When dinner was over, they helped their mother clear the table then went into the living room and turned on the television.

"Unbelievable! Now we have to put up with some stuck-up cousins we don't even remember. They're probably boring, too. I can see them now, criticizing everything because they're used to completely different things."

"Come on! We don't even know them. Maybe they're cool," Tony said, unconvinced. He was thirteen, calm and understanding, with dark hair and brown eyes, though not as tanned as his brother.

"I doubt it. I'll see to it that they leave soon."

"Don't be silly. Don't let Mom hear you say that either."

Their mother came into the room, wiping her hands with a dish cloth. "Have you brushed your teeth? Which one of you is cleaning the dishes?"

Tony grinned. He took the cloth from her hands, hit his brother's back with it and ran after him to the bathroom. Their mother followed them, laughing.

"When are our cousins coming?"

"Tomorrow, late in the afternoon."

"So soon?! Doesn't it seem too sudden to you?" Tony asked.

She looked at her eldest son, thinking.

"Now that you mention it, I think so, too. I wonder why. I hope Michael's not in trouble."

"What an idea, imposing his children on someone else like that," Daniel observed, in a bad mood and with his mouth full of toothpaste foam. "They must be really boring!"

She frowned. "You mustn't talk like that about your cousins, Daniel. I hope you get on well while they're here. What happened a few years ago was enough!"

"What happened? I don't remember them being here."

"When the four of you were playing, Daniel went behind Cousin Beatrix and bam! He cut her braids. She used to wear long braids. Now she looked like a boy. She was furious! She kept hitting Daniel. You were such a pest when you were little. Always up to no good."

Tony snickered, picturing the scene. Even his brother smiled, although he soon tried to disguise it.

"How old are they, mom?"

"Let me see. Christopher—Chris—is just a few months older than you. His sister must be twelve."

Daniel looked annoyed. Just his luck! He was the youngest of the four. Tony winked at his mother. He knew what was on his brother's mind.

"I want you to be kind to them. Are you listening, Daniel?"

He nodded. He kept thinking about it after his brother and his mother went to the kitchen. The idea of having two strangers in his house, having to share everything and not being able to say or do whatever he wanted was getting on his nerve. He probably wouldn't be able to spend the whole day at the beach as he used to do to keep his wretched cousins' company. So much for them! Serves them right, for coming out of the blue like that!

The next day, they woke up early and went for a swim in the sea, which was just awesome, with loads of waves, as Daniel used to say.

They had always lived in Nazaré and took pride in it. They only regretted being further away from the beach now than they used to up to a couple of years before. The old place was just a stone's throw from the beach. They'd fall asleep and wake up feeling the pleasant smell of salt air.

Now they lived in a very recent neighborhood far from the town center, much to the despair of both, who'd spend all the time in the sea as soon as the sun began to shine. Their mother was delighted.

The house they had moved into was like a palace compared to the previous one, which was a tiny little doll's house, as she said. She missed the old neighborhood, though.

After lunch, they laid down on the grass in the garden on their back with their hands folded under their heads.

"Aren't you a bit curious to meet our cousins, Daniel? They're almost as old as we are."

Daniel made a clicking sound with his lips. He was still a bit sulky. "Well, the boy must be cool. As for the girl—they're all pests!"

His brother laughed. "You'll change your mind a year or two from now!"

Daniel looked at him with a frown. He was silent for a few moments.

"Let's ride to the campsite and visit Rick and Jack. We haven't seen them since last summer. I'd like to be with them again. They must be all settled in by now," Tony said. His eyes were shining. "I wish I were in their shoes. Going camping without their parents—a dozen boys and only one adult, who by the way is cool and they hardly even notice. What can be better? That's the dream!"

"I'm not sure we should go there. The others may not like it."

"Get out of here! We know most of them. They came from Santarém with their families and rented beach tents here last summer."

"I know that. They don't care about me because I'm younger than they are. It sucks being the youngest!"

Tony laughed and gave him a friendly push.

"Come on! You can be such a killjoy! We won't be able to do it once our cousins are here. We don't know if they'll be willing to do it, too."

"Okay... Okay. Get the bikes. I'll tell mom."

They were riding their bikes on the road a few minutes later. They enjoyed breathing in the scent of pine trees while they chatted. They were feeling hot after a while.

"Here we are!"

"That was quick!"

They went through the gate and parked their bikes against a wall. Two bikes were already there, chained to each other with a strong lock.

"Whose bikes can those be?" Daniel asked, ringing the bells as if there was no tomorrow.

Tony nearly dragged him away. "The owners must be loaded! Come on. Jack's outside that blue tent."

"RICK! Look! Daniel and Tony are here!" a freckled boy shouted when he saw them.

Another young man, with disheveled hair, came out of the next tent, digging into a sandwich so hard it looked like he hadn't had anything to eat for at least two weeks.

"Daniel! Tony! We didn't know you were coming, did we, Jack?" Rick asked, taking a big bite of the sandwich. His friend nodded.

The brothers smiled, delighted with the reception they received, which pleased even serious-looking Daniel.

"Do you want to have a bite?"

"At half past three?" Daniel asked, startled.

"You're always hungry when you're camping. It's the smell of pine trees and salt air put together," Rick replied, smiling, and showing his jagged teeth.

"I'm so jealous! You just do what you want. No one tells you what to do."

The others agreed, pleased.

"To be honest, I'm hungry too. It must have been all the cycling," Tony said in a good mood. "You won't believe the news we have for you!"

Chapter 2

Bea, Chris... and Jack

"This sucks! Why do we have to visit some stupid cousins we've never met? Dad had a terrible idea!" said a tall, thin twelve-year-old girl with short, curly golden-brown hair and very beautiful light green eyes. A few freckles splashed her upturned nose and made her look friendly. Still, she was sulky as she gave her brother a quick look.

They hurried onto the train, avoiding the jostling of more impatient people. A crow was on the girl's shoulder. His black feathers shone so much that sometimes, when the sunlight hit it, they had blue or green hues that made him look fascinating. His eyes were bright with wit and his beak was long and strong. He was talking to his owner, pecking her softly in the ear.

Bea's countenance softened as if by magic. She scratched his head. "Crazy bird!"

The crow gave a loud laugh, perfectly mimicking the children's Dad. The people they came across stopped, amazed, when they realized it was the crow that was laughing so outrageously. They followed them with their gaze, smiling.

The bird, realizing he was the subject of so many people's amazement, laughed again, even more loudly.

«Hel-lo! Hel-lo!» he greeted, raising his head as he said «Hel» and lowering it as he said «lo», as if he was bowing to the audience.

The passengers smiled, fascinated by the bird's cleverness. They couldn't take their eyes off him.

"Well, waddya know?" a man said, scratching his head. "A talking crow! If anyone told me about it, I wouldn't believe it! Waddya know?"

«Well, waddya know? Well, waddya know?» said the crow, mimicking his voice perfectly, much to his delight and amazement.

Bea giggled. She was used to that kind of situation.

"Shush, you naughty boy! Shut up!"

«Shush, you naughty boy! Shut up! Shshshshshsh!»

Everyone laughed once more, amused.

Chris pushed his sister ahead of him, impatient. He was not as fond of mingling with strangers as she—who made friends just like that—was. Not him. He kept himself to himself. People wrongly thought he was unfriendly. His hair was blond, with very fair skin and blue eyes.

He flipped the bird's beak gently, trying to shut him up so he wouldn't attract so much attention.

«Naughty boy! Naughty boy!» he said, mimicking the boy's voice.

Chris smiled. "You'd better shut him up, or everyone will try to be next to us. Then we won't have a minute's peace!"

The girl grinned and patted the bird. "My darling Jack! I'm glad Dad didn't stop us from bringing it. I wouldn't leave without him anyway!"

Her brother shook his head disapprovingly. "You're just as crazy as Jack is! Does Aunt Christine know he's coming, too?"

"I don't know. I hope so."

"You must keep an eye on him all the time. You know what he's like with strangers. He'll start pecking everyone."

She turned to the bird and scratched the top of his head. "He'll behave very well, won't you, Jack?"

«Shush! Naughty boy!»

They laughed. They found an empty compartment and went in. They put down their backpacks and sat facing each other.

"Don't you think Dad looked strange when he spoke with us yesterday? I thought he was hiding something. What can it be?" Chris said, placing the backpacks on the luggage rack.

"I thought so, too. He sounded very mysterious when he was on the phone with Godmom. He shooed me out of the room when he saw me and told me off. He's never kept anything from us before. Something very strange must be going! Lately I caught him whispering something to Mom a few times. They shut up as soon as they saw me!"

"Then, out of the blue, he decided to send us to stay with Aunt Christine. He promised he'd take us to Morocco. Yeah, right!"

Their father was a cruise ship captain. He had traveled all over the world. They thought he was lucky.

"It's like he couldn't wait to get rid of us," Bea said, sorrowful. She really loved her father. "He nearly forced us to get on the train, bikes and all!"

Her brother chuckled. "You'd think he made us carry them on our back!"

Bea looked at him, annoyed. "You know perfectly well what I mean! Stop being so boring!"

«Boring! Naughty boy! Well, waddya know?»

They laughed. Sometimes, the crow seemed to understand what was going on and said the right word at the right time.

"I didn't like being treated as if we were little children either, when he warned us not to talk to strangers," said Bea, who knew her own mind.

Her brother was thinking. "Dad was definitely worried about something. He doesn't usually do that. Mom seemed more distracted than usual, too. Her mind seemed to be miles away."

A few minutes later, they were already hungry. They took out the snack their mother had packed for them. They unwrapped cheese and ham sandwiches and tasted them, delighted, with the help of the crow, who seemed to be as hungry as they were.

"I hadn't realized I was so hungry!" the boy said, taking a huge bite of the sandwich. "Bea, do something! That greedy Jack took out a huge piece of cheese!"

«Greedy! Greedy! Naughty boy!» said Jack, dropping the cheese on the seat, then picking it up again with his beak and moving a bit further away from Chris, afraid he would take it away. He was a very sly bird indeed!

"The poor thing must be as hungry as we are!" said the girl, handing a pack of juice to her brother. "What do you think the cousins will be like, Chris?"

"I don't know. I have absolutely no idea. They'll probably be a quarrelsome, impolite bunch. We'd better not give them any confidence. We don't really have to spend the whole day with them."

His sister silently agreed as she finished eating. She got up a little later. "I'm going to the toilet. Please see to it that Jack doesn't follow me."

Jack suddenly realized his beloved owner wasn't there. He let out an indignant cry when Chris grabbed him firmly. Jack pecked him and was immediately released.

"You rascal! Wait till I get you. I'll flick you in the beak. You nasty bird!"

Jack hopped out of the compartment with a mocking laugh, mimicking the words he had just learned. There was no sign of his little owner in the hallway, much to its disappointment. He saw the door to the next compartment was open, so he went inside, determined to see if she was hiding there.

A half toothless old lady with a very hairy moustache was sitting sound asleep, snoring with her mouth open. There was a large basket full of overripe apples and pears on her lap.

Jack flew to a luggage rack and hid behind a brown bag. He cocked his head, looked at her with great interest and mimicked her snoring perfectly. Then he coughed softly as the street sweeper used to do. She didn't even notice him. Jack wasn't used to this, so he coughed harder.

«Hel-lo! Hel-lo! HEL-LO!»

Not only did she not wake up, but she also snored even louder. Jack paced impatiently. He didn't like being ignored like that. The nerve of the woman!

Suddenly, he remembered what the children's father used to say to wake up his daughter.

«Wake up, you lazy girl! Wake up, you lazy girl! WAKE UP!» he shouted, staring at her.

She woke up. She was so startled the basket fell to the floor. There was fruit all over the place. She looked around, a little dazed, not knowing what had woken her.

"Oh, dear! What have you done!"

«Oh, dear! What have you done!»

She looked around, confused. Was there an echo in the train? She bent down to pick up the fruit, a little suspicious.

«Rascal! You naughty boy! What have you done! Oh, dear!»

She dropped the pears she was holding and looked around, alarmed. Where did that disembodied voice come from?

Jack giggled, amused by the situation.

The poor lady was bled white. Her legs were shaking as she stood up. She didn't dare to look around, afraid she might find a demonic being having fun at her expense. She sat down slowly and gradually went back to her own self. How silly of her! She must be hearing things. She just needed a rest!

There was a meow. Then another more prolonged, almost distressing meow.

She certainly wasn't expecting that. A cat! A cat meowing on a train! Poor little thing! Who would be cruel enough to abandon a cat?! She started to look under the seats, convinced she was going to find it. To no avail. She peeked into the hallway, but all she saw was a man looking out the window.

She went back inside and picked the fruit from the floor. It was hard for her to be on her knees.

Jack was watching her very attentively, cocking his head.

Suddenly he growled menacingly. The old lady dropped the basket again, terrified. She looked around, eyes almost popping out of their sockets, and ran out, slipping on an apple and nearly charging at the man by the window.

She entered the first door she saw. She sat down, talking to herself and staring at the door, terrified at the prospect of whatever it was that made those noises coming for her. She was shivering and was as white as snow.

Chris looked at her, surprised. He wondered what had scared her fellow passenger so much. He looked out the window, afraid she might start a conversation. He was definitely not in the mood for chatting.

Bea was in the hallway on her way back from the toilet when she saw the old lady hurrying out of the compartment. She peered at the place she had come from, curious. She saw the fruit scattered on the floor. Jack landed on her shoulder, startling her.

«Naughty boy! Naughty boy! Rascal!»

"You little pest! You scared that poor lady! Shame on you! Bad boy!" she scolded him and flicked him in the beak. She picked up the fruit, put it in the basket as best she could and returned to her compartment, carrying the basket with some difficulty. She chuckled when she saw the frightened face of the owner of the basket and handed it to her. "I apologize if my crow scared you. He isn't usually so cheeky. My name's Bea and this is Jack. That's my brother Chris."

The old lady looked at her, amazed, watching the bird intently. "Goodness gracious! Was that him making all that noise?! Well, I never! He gave me quite a scare!"

Jack looked at her with his bright eyes and greeted her with a bow as he often did, much to everyone's amusement.

«Hel-lo! Hel-lo!»

"What a smart bird! It sounds like someone speaking. It would never cross my mind. Well, waddya know?"

Bea smiled, satisfied with the compliment she had paid to her beloved crow.

«Well, waddya know? Well, waddya know?» Jack said, delighted by the sound of the new words.

The rest of the journey was quite fun and pleasant. The old lady kept messing around with the bird and gave him an apple and a pear. She didn't even care he pecked half a dozen more. Chris was not part of the general joy. He couldn't hide the fact that he was annoyed at such an unexpected voyage.

If he only knew what awaited them.

Chapter 3

A rather inauspicious beginning

"We're there!" Bea announced, looking out the window. She observed the station and smiled. "This is Pataias! Let's go!"

Her brother got up in a bad mood and shooed the crow away. Jack seemed determined to remove the laces from his sneakers.

«Naughty boy! Rascal!»

They laughed and got off the train, carrying their backpacks. Their traveling companion got off in Martingança, much to their relief. She had proved to be quite talkative.

They waited for their bikes to disembark and hopped on them, pedaling slowly.

"I could do with an ice cream. It's so hot!" Bea observed, huffing and puffing with all the heat. Jack was flying beside her. He landed on her head every once in a while, which made her laugh.

"Look! A pastry shop!"

They got off their bikes, leaned them against the entrance and went in. They came out shortly afterwards, discouraged.

"No ice cream! Can you believe it?"

"Stop grumbling! Let's go to that café over there. They must sell ice creams there!"

They pedaled a bit more and headed for the counter. An overweight man with a thick mustache and shiny eyes smiled at them.

"You look like you want ice cream, if I'm not mistaken," he said. He took an interested look at the bird that accompanied them. To his surprise, Jack mimicked his laughter. "Well, well!"

«Well, well! Well, well! Well, whaddya know?» Jack said, adding a very loud snort.

"A pineapple juice and a strawberry cone, please."

He waited on them without pretending not to be surprised at the bird. "An aunt of mine had a crow who could speak—not as good as yours, of course. Many people were fooled by him, truth be told."

«Hel-lo! Hel-lo! Naughty boy! Rascal! Well, well!»

The waiter burst out laughing. Two customers who were sitting in the corner drinking beer did the same.

"It's always the same with you, wherever you go!" Chris said, shaking his head. "You should taste the ice cream, Bea. Don't just devour it!"

"It's so good! I was so thirsty!"

"Ice cream doesn't quench your thirst. Quite the opposite."

"Come on! You're only saying that because you don't like it! You must be the only person I know who doesn't like ice cream!"

«Come on! Well, well! Well, whaddya know?» Jack said, ending with a big sneeze. Everybody laughed.

"Maybe we should get going. Soon enough the whole town will be here, marveling at Jack!" Chris commented with a chuckle.

They paid and went out, much to the pity of those who remained, who were delighted with the bird's cleverness. Jack continued to shout silly things, which made them giggle.

Pataias was behind them shortly afterwards. They cycled in single file. Chris was leading the way. They took a deep breath of the pine forest air and almost forgot that they did not want to make that trip.

"Do you think we're still far from the campsite?"

"Probably not. We must be near it. Mind you, I sure they'll let you in. Do you remember what they said i. letters? No girls allowed, says the monitor. I guess you'll have to wait by the gate."

Bea frowned angrily. "If you think I'll stay outside while you're having fun with Paul and Louie, you're crazy!"

"Everyone will know you're a girl. There's no way you can disguise it!"

"We'll see about that," she said as she stopped by the roadside and got off the bike quickly.

She rubbed her hands on the floor and then on her face. She took a cap from her backpack, put it on her head and pulled it almost down to her eyes.

"Auntie will have a fit when she sees you looking so dirty!" Chris said, laughing out loud. The crow imitated his laugh.

"Who's going to stop me from joining you now?"

They got to the campsite a few minutes later. They left their bikes near the entrance after asking for information.

"It's so big! I never thought it would be like this. It has such an interesting name, too: Paradise Valley.

"I wish Dad had let us camp with them instead of sending us to stay with perfect strangers," Chris said, frowning. "Look, there's Louie and Paul! HI!"

«Hel-lo! Hel-lo!»

They ran towards a red tent, excited. They all shouted happily. Then they sat on the floor in a circle, chatting. The crow would join in whenever possible, snorting, which made them laugh in return. They ended up having lunch together, sharing food and chatting the afternoon away.

Four boys were talking in front of a nearby tent. They could barely hear each other.

"Hey, you! Stop that racket! You're not the only ones around here, you know?" Tony shouted disapprovingly.

"Yeah!" Jack agreed, swallowing his food quickly. They're not usually like that. It must be those two in jeans that are making such a fuss! They came to visit them."

Bea, Chris, Louie and Paul looked at each other, snickering.

"Shut up, Jack! Hush!" the little girl scolded him, flicking him in the beak softly. The crow was making most of the noise.

«Shut up, Jack! Hush!» he said. Then he laughed mockingly.

Jack made a disapproving gesture. He thought the rude reply had come from one of the boys he didn't know.

"How dare you? You shut up!"

«YOU SHUT UP, you idiot!» shouted Jack before he burst out laughing. He took off, landed on top of the tent, and strolled from one end to the other.

The boys jumped. The other boys' laughter had angered them even more. They couldn't help it. Daniel's brother wasn't able to stop him, who had a terrible temper, from coming towards them. Daniel pushed Bea, whom he thought was the one who had made fun of him.

She jumped, furious, and punched him right in the jaw, taking him by surprise. He landed on the floor. Tony came to his brother's aid. He moved towards the "boy" to ask "him" why "he" had done that to his brother.

Suddenly, he too was lying on the floor. The "boy" in the cap snorted. "He" laughed so much "he" nearly fell off. "He" just couldn't stop.

Daniel got up, angry, feeling his chin. It was sore. He moved towards "him", but the blond boy stood in front of him.

"No fighting!" Chris said firmly.

"I wasn't talking to you, dude!"

"That doesn't matter. I won't let you do it."

Tony stood before him, frowning.

Chris was not intimidated by his height. He kept his gaze steady. "That is, unless you're used to punching girls…"

The other boys looked at each other, astonished, then at the little girl who looked like she was about to hurl herself at them, clenched fists and green eyes sparkling.

"That's true. Bea's his sister. We've been friends for a long time," Louie said, taking off his cap.

Daniel looked at her menacingly. "What if I punch a girl? Didn't she punch us, too?" he asked, indignant.

The others laughed. He was even more furious.

"Don't forget it was you who started!" Chris remarked, smiling.

"You were rude to Jack!" Tony said, frowning.

"No, we weren't. None of us made fun of you. Blame *him!*" Paul said, still laughing. "It's Bea's crow. His name's Jack, too."

They all turned and looked at the bird, which was still on top of the tent. Jack cocked his head, as if he were very interested in the conversation.

"My sister told him to shut up. He just repeated what he had heard. The little rascal does it all the time!"

«Naughty boy! Rascal! Fool! Well, whaddya know?» Jack said, bursting out laughing.

The four stared at him, gaping. They had never thought a crow would be able to speak like that.

"I'm glad I didn't punch you," Tony said, relieved. "I could have hurt you."

"If I'd let you do it, that is," Bea replied, disdainful.

"There, there! Don't you start again!" Chris, who hated arguments, said.

"This camp is for boys only. How did they let you in?" Daniel asked, giving her an angry look.

"If you complain about me, I'll... I'll punch you again!" Bea threatened, furious.

A thin man with thick hair, wearing shorts and a T-shirt, approached them, looking serious. He had noticed the fight and was not happy. Chris pulled his sister's cap on her head and stood in front of her. The bird flew to her shoulder and started pecking her cap, chattering something nobody understood.

"What's all this about?" he asked, inspecting the newcomers. His gaze lingered on Bea and her strange companion.

"It was just a misunderstanding caused by our friends' crow, Mr. Ferdinand. You won't believe it. It can talk like a person, not like a parrot. It can do people's voices perfectly," Louie told him, laughing.

He looked at the bird doubtfully.

«Hel-lo! Hel-lo! Well, whaddya know? Rascal! Naughty boy!» Jack said, bowing—he knew everybody liked that.

Mr. Ferdinand let out a roaring laugh, which the bird mimicked perfectly, causing everyone's laughter and attracting other boys, who came by and stared at the bird, surprised.

When he saw there were so many people watching him, Jack presented them with a monumental sneeze, followed by a hideous, deep, cavernous cough, which he had heard from a tramp. He ended with some meowing.

"I knew crows are smart and learn from experience. I didn't know they could speak that well!" Mr. Ferdinand said, surprised. "You have a beautiful bird, kid. Just don't stay for long around here."

He walked away, smiling at their astonishment. The children looked at each other, not knowing what to say. Then Chris turned to Tony and nodded. "Thanks for keeping your mouths shut."

Daniel and Bea looked at each other, frowning. They disliked each other and they both wanted to fight.

"That's one amazing bird you got there," Tony said, a little embarrassed by the other boy's thanks.

«Naughty boy! Rascal! Well, whaddya know?» the crow said, jumping to his owner's shoulder. They laughed and returned to their tents.

"We're leaving. We still have to look for our Uncle and Aunt's house. We'll be staying with them for a few days. You don't know how lucky you are!" Chris commented, envious. "We'll be back here as soon as we can."

They went to fetch their bikes. They noticed the other bikes and guessed who they belonged to. They were on their way a few moments later. Jack was flying beside them.

"We must be going, too. We'll come back some other day," said Tony, leaving.

They put their T-shirts on and got on their bikes.

"That girl's a real pest!" said Daniel, touching his chin. "And a mean puncher, too!"

"I'm glad we'll never see them again, Daniel!"

Tony couldn't be more wrong.

Chapter 4

A very strange attitude

Tony and Daniel pushed the gate that led to the small garage and parked their bikes. Then they ran to the door and went in. They were starving. As they passed the living room, they froze, stunned. Bea and Chris were pleasantly chatting with their mother, looking like they had known each other forever.

"YOU?!"

Their mother looked astonished at her children and her nephews. She realized they all looked displeased. "Have you met?" she asked. Suddenly, she laughed, amused. "Don't tell me Tony and Daniel are the naughty boys you were talking about!"

Jack mimicked her laughter, which made her laugh even more. Bea and Chris looked down in embarrassment. Tony smiled, amused by the situation, whereas his brother frowned, furious.

"I don't understand where all the fun is, Mom!" Daniel said. He was increasingly sulky. He felt his aching chin again. "She was the rude one."

"There, there. Why don't you forget everything that happened and try to become friends? After all, you'll be living under the same roof for a while. It was just an unfortunate misunderstanding. You'll end up seeing eye to eye—at least that's what your Godmother says," his mother said with a little smile. They looked confused, which made her laugh again. "My sister is Bea's godmother, as well as Daniel's."

The two younger children couldn't disguise their annoyance. Not only did they dislike each other, but they also shared the same godmother. That had really ruined the rest of the day.

"Come have a snack! You must be hungry. I baked an orange cake that looks delicious. You better take a shower first, Bea. You don't look very clean," she observed, smiling. "Your room's upstairs. You can put your backpacks there. The bathroom is across the hallway."

"How will I know which room was meant for me and which one's my brother's?"

"That's easy. It's the one with bunk beds and no clothes lying all over the place. My children aren't exactly what you'd call tidy."

The children moved away in embarrassment. They washed their hands in the ground floor bathroom. Then it was their cousin's turn. They were uncomfortable, which made them seem even more clumsy. They kept bumping into each other. Then they went into the kitchen. Their mother was staring at the table, looking puzzled.

"What's wrong, Mom?" Tony asked, curious. He was rubbing his hands. There was so much delicious food on the table! Bottles of cold juice, ham and cheese sandwiches, jello, flan, chocolate mousse: everything they liked. Their appetite grew even more.

"I seem to have misplaced my cake," she confessed, increasingly disconcerted.

Her children laughed, much to their cousin's surprise. He was even more surprised when he saw her peeking under the sink, into the fridge, the stove, and the washing machine.

"She isn't looking for the cake in there, is she?"

Daniel and Tony couldn't help laughing out loud, surprising their cousin.

"Mom's very absent-minded. She sometimes puts things in the strangest places. We laugh our heads off because of it!"

Tony said, laughing, as he started to look for the cake, too. "What were you doing the last time you saw the cake, Mom?"

"Let's see. I remember unmolding it and thinking it had turned out right this time. I was placing it on the table when I remembered to put fresh towels in the bathroom upstairs in case your cousins wanted to take a shower as soon as they got here."

Daniel let out a loud laugh. "Then you know where it is, Mom. In the bathroom!"

She chuckled, then ran up the stairs. Bea was already there, peeking out as she made her way. That must be Uncle and Aunt's bedroom. Another double bedroom. A smaller one with two dark wooden bunk beds, which had to be her cousins' bedroom—it looked like a hurricane had passed through.

"Man! If our bedrooms ever looked like this, we'd live on bread and water for two weeks! Poor Auntie!"

The next room was about the same size as the previous one. There were bunk beds, too—iron ones, painted red. She opened the closet and sucked in the air, pleased with the smell that came from it. Several hangers awaited their clothes. She put their backpacks there, taking out only the clothes and shoes she would wear after showering. They would deal with the rest of the clothes later.

She went to the bathroom opposite and closed the door behind her. The first thing that caught her attention was a plate with a delicious-looking cake on a small white chest of drawers. It seemed to be a little out of place there.

"What a strange place for a cake! Maybe it's a local thing—a weird one, at that!"

There was a knock on the door.

"Bea! It's me. Is there a cake there, by any chance?"

"As a matter of fact, there is, Aunt Christine. You may come in."

She entered, trying hard not to laugh. "You must think we're crazy. You see, I keep misplacing things. I came here to bring clean towels, and I brought the cake that I had just unmolded.

You won't believe the crazy things I sometimes do! I've been looking for that cake all over the place. Don't take too long, otherwise there will be nothing left when you come downstairs."

Bea smiled. She really liked her distracted aunt, who could laugh at herself and find the situations she got into as funny as everybody else did. She came down ten minutes later, as fresh as a daisy, spotless and beautiful. She was a different person.

As soon as he saw her, Jack jumped from Chris's shoulder to that of his beloved owner. «Hel-lo! Hel-lo! Well, whaddya know?»

Her aunt smiled, pleased with the way she looked. She watched her children's reaction out of the corner of her eye. Daniel gaped, surprised, but immediately closed his mouth, so that no one would notice his surprise.

"You look... different," Tony said, nearly choking. "Zaza rang. She asked us to go and see her as soon as we finish eating."

His cousins looked at him, astonished. "Zaza?!"

Tony scratched his head in embarrassment. "Well, that's what I call her ever since I was little. I never got used to calling her Aunt. It's silly, but I can't call her any other way."

"I don't think it's stupid. I call her Zazabeth," Chris said.

Everyone laughed. They said goodbye to Christine, who went to the door, pleased. As they left the gate, they almost ran into a thin man wearing light pants and a striped shirt, whose thin face made his long nose stand out even more. He was a little bald and wore round-rimmed glasses. He greeted them with a nod and went inside. Bea watched him, distracted. She didn't even notice that the three boys were looking at her, puzzled.

"What's wrong, Bea?"

"I'm not sure. I think I've seen his face somewhere before. Where was it?"

"I don't think you've ever seen him before. We've just arrived," Chris said, watching him.

"Maybe he wants to rent the other room. Mom usually rents a room in the summer. Now, let's go!"

They left. The crow was flying beside them, shouting some of the words he knew, amusing everyone. Even Daniel would giggle now and then. He liked the bird much more than he liked Jack's owner, and he envied her for it. As they went by the harbor, Tony pointed to his father and his grandfather's ships, which were close to each other. They cycled a little more. As they came out of a curve, they saw a charming-looking one-storey house a little above the road. It was being restored. Stonemasons and painters were at work, busy.

They got off and pushed the bikes up the hill. It was no easy task. The wheels kept getting buried in the sand. Two old fig trees and a pine forest stood behind the house. Birds sang at the top of their lungs, provoking Jack, who mimicked them and made them speechless.

"It used to be the ranger's house. Zaza fell in love with it the first time she saw it, even in ruins. She sold her apartment and decided to restore it inside and out."

Bea's eyes were shining like stars. "It's beautiful! It makes me feel—I don't even know how to say it!"

Daniel laughed out loud. "That's what my Godmom says. She said she was in love the first time she set her eyes on it. She didn't know why. Many people said she was crazy."

"It really looks cool," Chris said. The others agreed.

They turned and stopped before the house, admiring the simple, pleasant lines, with many doors and sash windows.

A blond, mischievous-looking seven-year-old boy came running, screaming, pretending to be terrified. He was being chased by a dark-haired two-year-old girl with beautiful blue eyes, who laughed heartily as she pedaled furiously on a tricycle, trying to catch him.

The little girl stopped pedaling when she saw the visitors. She smiled delightedly to those she knew. She couldn't help noticing the crow on Bea's shoulder.

"Hi! What's his name?"

«Hel-lo! Hel-lo!»

The little girl burst out laughing, drawing the attention of her brother, who came out of nowhere and threw himself into Tony's arms.

"His name is Jack, Agnes. I'm Bea and this is Chris."

"Oh!" she exclaimed, looking very serious. "I'll call Mom. She's watching that man—working."

She left, pedaling swiftly.

"I thought you'd never come!" the little one said. His eyes shone bright. He shook hands with them happily, jumping up and down in the process. "I've been watching the men paint. I'd like to paint, too, but they won't let me."

The cousins laughed and headed for the door. A lady who looked a lot like the boys' mother—if only a bit younger—ran towards them, smiling, and kissed them all affectionately.

"I thought you'd got lost! Hello, Jack!" she exclaimed, smiling. She turned and looked at the house, eyes shining. "So, do you like it?"

"It's beautiful, Godmom!"

"Mom and Dad send you their love, Zazabeth."

She laughed. She had always liked the way the two boys used to call her. "Michael sent something for me, didn't he?"

Bea and Chris looked at each other and shook their heads.

"Oh! Okay then. Have a look inside. Park your bikes over there. I'll be with you in a moment."

The four of them got inside, together with the children.

As he saw his aunt was not following them, Tony went back. What he saw left him speechless. Chris noticed his strange countenance and peeked out, too. He, too, was surprised.

She had crouched down next to Bea's bicycle and looked around cautiously. She searched with her hands under the saddle. After a few moments, she took out a little square, flat package wrapped in brown paper and attached to the inside of the saddle with brown adhesive tape, the kind that is usually used in parcels. She put the package in a pocket in her shorts and stood up. Her cheeks were flushed.

The boys gasped. They didn't know what to think of her strange attitude. The thought that some precious item had been smuggled crossed their minds, but they shook their heads. What a ridiculous idea! As Zaza joined them, she noticed the two boys' fleeting look, then she looked brightly outside, realizing that they must have seen her. She chuckled.

"I hope you're not thinking Michael's been smuggling something!" she said, smiling. They blushed, which made her burst out laughing. "Oh! So that's exactly what you thought! Well, I'd better tell you, so you won't misjudge both of us! But I'll only tell you two. I need you to keep it a secret. Your father was given a very important object on his last trip. He was asked to keep it safe. The owner of the object thought he was being followed. Michael thought he was being followed soon afterwards. He was afraid someone would steal it, so he sent it for me to hide it in a safe place until he asks it back. No one would suspect our little conspiracy—except you now, of course. You must promise you won't say a word about it to anyone. Not even your brother and sister. It's not that I don't trust them. You see, Daniel has a terrible temper. He might end up spilling the beans. Bea would see spies everywhere. I want her to spend a few pleasant days here, with no worries."

The boys looked at each other knowingly. They were also proud an adult had trusted them enough to tell them such a mysterious secret. Their eyes were bright with excitement.

Their aunt understood and smiled. "Isn't it exciting? Now, don't be suspicious of all the strangers! Of course, if you feel that someone is following you, or that they seem very interested in Bea and you, Chris, let me know and don't give away any information. Now, come with me. Don't worry! Nothing's going to happen. You'll have a very peaceful vacation. You'll see!"

Little did she know how wrong she was.

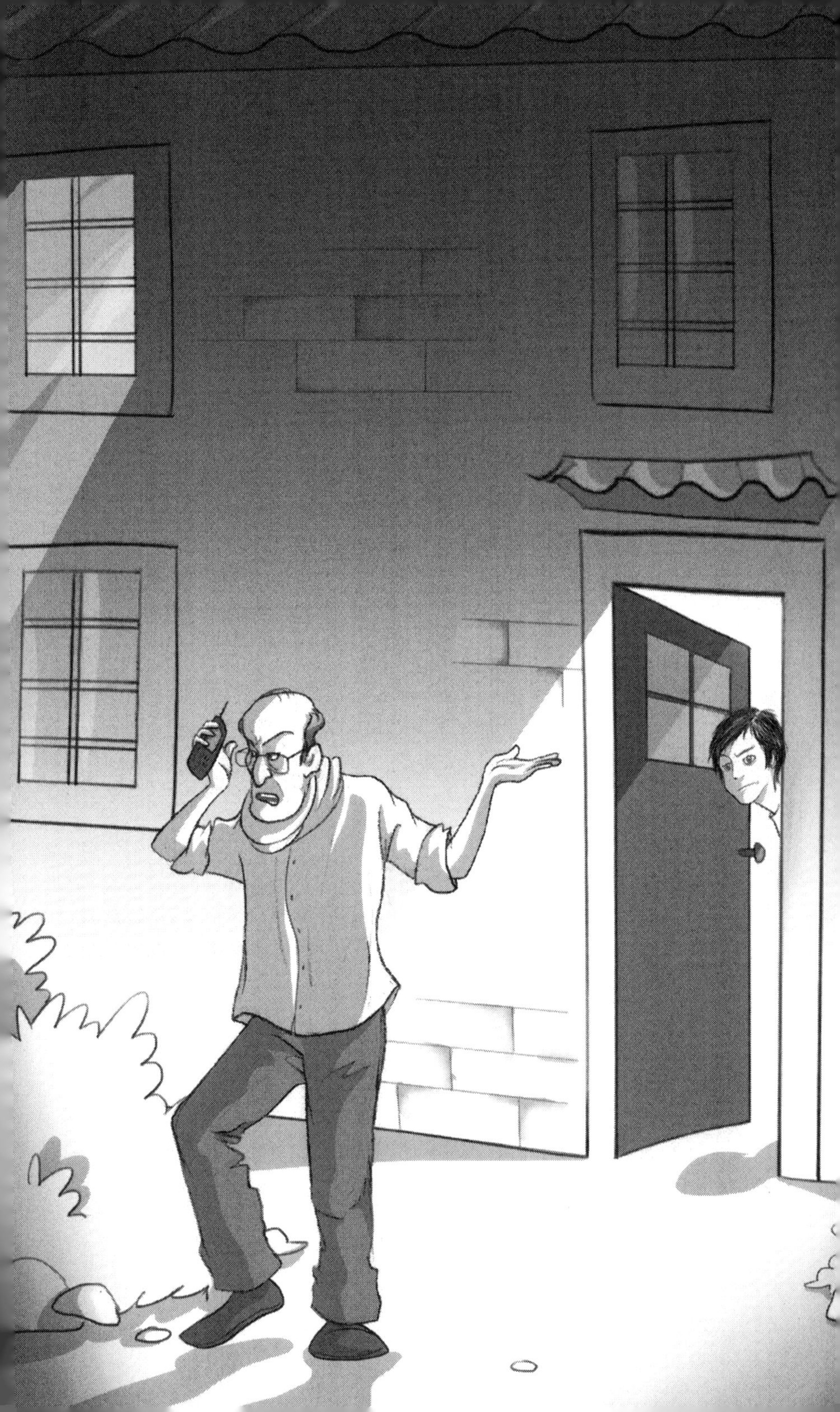

Chapter 5

A very suspicious lodger and a funny prank

The four cousins got home eager to have dinner. They were starving, maybe because of all the cycling. Tony and Daniel ran in, unlike the other two. As they passed by the living room, they saw someone sitting in front of the television, watching the news. They went into the kitchen. Christine was stirring something in a huge pot. It smelled wonderful. Their mouths watered, and their eyes widened when they saw a huge Molotof egg white pudding on the counter.

"Hi! Back so soon? How was the outing? Is construction going well?" she asked, smiling. She was very flushed. She ran her hands over her cheeks. "It's so hot in here!"

«Hel-lo! Hel-lo! Well, whaddya know?»

She laughed and gave the bird a piece of bread.

"Who's that, Mom?" Tony asked, running his finger over the egg cream topping and subsequently licking it with delight.

His cousins watched him, appalled. Daniel tried to do the same, but this time his mother saw it and slapped his hand.

"Nobody touches the pudding before dinner! He's the new lodger. He'll be staying for a couple of nights. He asked me if he could watch the news. I said yes, of course."

Daniel twitched his nose, annoyed. He gave his brother an angry, jealous look. His brother gave him a wry smile. The sight of that bright yellow pudding was all he could think of.

"Do you need any help, Aunt Christine?" Chris asked, much to his cousins' amazement. They were unable to hide their surprise. It had never crossed their minds to do the same.

Aunt Christine smiled at him, pleased. "Thank you, Chris. Can you prepare the salad? Everything you need is in the sink."

Suddenly, a booming voice made them jump. The new lodger was there. No one had heard his footsteps.

"Are all these children yours, Mrs. Ricardo?"

"Heavens, no! Two of them are mine. The other two are my nephews who came to spend a few days here. I hadn't seen them in ages," she said, smiling as she stirred the pot again.

The man stared at Bea and Chris and nodded. "So? Do you like it here?"

"Yes, sir."

Tony gave him a suspicious look. "How did you know it's them who are here on vacation?"

The man blinked quickly and looked at the boy. "Well, it occurred to me that you'd be Mrs. Ricardo's children because of the color of your hair. Oh, I'm sorry. I haven't told you my name yet. I'm Balthazar Gomes."

Bea looked intently at him. He raised his eyebrows. "I think I've seen you somewhere before. I just don't know where."

The boys noticed he startled a bit. He disguised as best he could. "That's not likely, kid. I only got here today."

"I'm sure I've seen your face quite recently," she insisted, trying hard to remember. "It'll come back to me anytime soon."

"What an interesting bird!" the lodger said, looking at him, curious, and raising his hand to pat it. Bea was unable to stop him.

Jack pecked his hand, tearing off a piece of skin from which blood came out. The man's eyes flashed menacingly. They all realized he had to stop himself from punching him.

"OUCH! Rascal! Naughty boy!" he scolded Jack, pretending to be in a good mood. Actually, it was quite the opposite. He wanted to twist the bird's neck. He squeezed his hand tightly to stop the blood flow. You could see he was in pain just by looking at his face.

"I apologize for Jack, Mr. Gomes. You see, he doesn't like strangers," Bea apologized awkwardly, flipping his beak. "You naughty boy! Don't do that!"

«Rascal! Naughty boy! Well, whaddya know?» Jack said, mimicking the lodger's voice and ending with a sneeze.

Mr. Gomes tried to smile. It didn't turn out well. Aunt Christine came to the rescue, a bit flustered, and took him to the bathroom to dress his wound. The boys looked at each other, worried. They were aware of their mother's embarrassment.

"You should control your bird! If it doesn't know how to behave, you should put it in a cage!" Daniel advised, frowning. "That's right: a CAGE!"

Bea was so angry she shivered and became very flushed. She clenched her fists and came close to her cousin's face looking so threateningly at him he had to back away.

"Don't you dare say such a cruel thing like that! Jack's never been in a cage—not even when he was little! He would die if I ever put him in a cage! What's more, he usually behaves himself! He just doesn't like it when strangers touch him, that's all! And, for your information, neither do I!"

"Come on! If you had taught it properly, it wouldn't have done what it did! You should send it away while you're here, Beatrix!" Daniel said. He went pale. Deep down he didn't think that way, but he found his cousin's attitude deeply irritating.

"Never! If he goes, I'll go, too! We are inseparable! We'll go to my parents', where we are welcome. And don't call me Beatrix! I hate that name!"

Her cousin smiled contemptuously. "As if your parents didn't try to impose you stuck-ups on us, Beatrix! Even they were dying to get rid of you! They couldn't stand you anymore! I wonder why!"

Their mother was now standing before them, staring at them very seriously. "That's enough, Daniel! This time you've said way too much. Now, go to your room. Don't get out without my permission."

"But, Mom! I was just—"

"I don't care. Go to your room and think about all the nasty things you said. It's high time you learned to think before you speak."

Daniel ran up the stairs, furious at being told off in front of his cousins. Drat! Exactly on the day when there was *Molotof* pudding for dessert. He slammed the door shut and threw himself on the bed, sulking. The mood wasn't much better downstairs. Chris and Tony were silent, not knowing what to say. Bea was trying very hard not to cry.

"Pay no attention to what he said, dear. He really didn't mean it! He doesn't think that way. He said all that nonsense because he was angry. He can be very impulsive, you know?"

"No, Aunt Christine. I know when I'm not welcome. Daniel's mad because we're here. He doesn't want us to be here! I wish I could go home!" she exclaimed, her eyes full of tears.

"Don't say that, Bea. You'll all get along eventually," her aunt said, looking insistently at her eldest son.

"Mom's right, Bea. That's just the way Daniel is. He says the first thing that comes to his mind and then he regrets it," he said, running his hand through his hair, embarrassed.

"You also made him do it, Bea."

She looked at her brother, angry, and sat up, a little sad. The crow started pulling her hair, as if realizing she needed support. "Well, I guess we should just forget about it. Let's have dinner."

"Aren't we going to wait for Uncle Julian?"

Their aunt smiled, shaking her head. "He's gone fishing. I hope he brings lots of fish."

The meal took place without incident. Aunt Christine tried to make the children feel at ease, telling them stories from her childhood, which she had spent with her sister, the children's father and his sister Mila, who also lived in Lisbon.

"Speaking of *Molotof* pudding, I'm going to tell you a story that happened to me, Mila and your Dad at your grandparents' house. We were all still single back then. My sister was a little girl. She laughed her head off," Christine said, giggling. Her eyes were shining as she recalled. "Your Granny had bought a *Molotof* pudding—perhaps it was someone's birthday. Michael was a very playful boy. He stuck his finger in it and challenged me to do the same. Then he started to knead it furiously. We all laughed our heads off—that is, except his mother, who didn't find it funny at all. I don't think we've ever had so much fun!"

Daniel heard laughter downstairs. He sulked even more. They were all having fun and stuffing themselves with pudding while he was there, staring at the ceiling. The little boy was beginning to think life was very cruel and unfair. Time went by. He was getting hungrier by the minute. He knew his mother would let him have dinner if he apologized to his cousin, but he was too proud to do it, although, deep down, he felt he had gone too far and deserved to be punished.

A bit later, he seemed to hear a noise by the door. He was expecting his brother to come in, but that didn't happen. Eventually he got up and opened the door slowly. Although he didn't see anyone, Oh, joy! A huge slice of pudding with egg cream all over it was at his feet in a bowl. He could hardly believe his eyes. He went back in and feasted on it, delighted, thanking his brother to himself. He hid the bowl under the bed, afraid his mother would tell his brother off if she found out he had broken the punishment.

A few hours later, everyone was in bed, sleeping, except Daniel, who could do with a bite. Tony slept soundly and made noises with his mouth from time to time, preventing him from sleeping.

He heard a noise, but he couldn't find out where it came from. The thought that his cousins might run away into the night crossed his mind. Now that would be great, he couldn't help thinking. He soon put the idea out of his mind. It wouldn't be good at all if it happened. Surely his mother would blame him for his cousins' flight.

Feeling a little uneasy, he got up and left the room, barefoot. He opened his cousins' bedroom door and took a quick look inside. They were both there, sleeping soundly. No wonder: their belly was full! He rubbed his belly and felt an unpleasant emptiness. It kept growling. Suddenly, he was terrified. Jack had landed on his shoulder. He had woken up when he entered the room. The crow whispered something in his ear. He liked that naughty kid.

The boy smiled and patted his head. "It's you, you rascal! You gave me quite a scare."

The lodger's door was ajar. He stuck his head in and peered. His eyes widened, surprised. There was no one there. He must have been the one who made the noise. Curious, Daniel went down the stairs. He had to find out why he had left his bedroom that late. He looked at his watch. The hands glowed in the dark. It was after one o'clock. He remembered one of his mother's rules: lodgers must be back by midnight. From then on, they were on their own. He noticed the kitchen door was ajar and headed towards it. Now he was really curious. He peeked and saw the lodger in the garden, holding his cell phone.

"That's strange! Why did he have to go outside to make a call?" he wondered, trying to listen. He had to know.

"I haven't had the chance yet. Yeah. As soon as possible. Don't worry. Yeah. I'm sure. I'll have to put up with those brats for another day or two."

Daniel looked at him. Now he was even more suspicious. Although he had no idea what he was talking about, he didn't like his tone of voice when he spoke about them. It had sounded very dangerous.

Suddenly, he smiled. He had an idea. He locked the door quietly and ran upstairs. There was laughter on his pesky face.

He waited at the top of the stairs. He soon realized that the man had exclaimed something, surprised as he tried to push the door open. The boy covered his mouth with his hands, so that his laughter could not be heard. The crow was still on his shoulder, tugging on his hair playfully. He patted his head, pleased to see the bird seemed to like him. He envied his cousin for the hundredth time for having a pet that was so fond of her and was that clever. He went back to bed and laughed softly, imagining the man's face when he found out he was locked outside. He even forgot how hungry he was and ended up falling asleep.

Outside, Mr. Gomes tried to open the door for the tenth time. He felt like punching someone. "Damn! One of the kids must have locked me outside. Rascal! If I ever find out which one of those pests did it! You don't know who you're messing with! Damn!"

At dawn, when Christine was going out to meet her husband at the harbor, she found the lodger sitting on a chair they used to sunbathe. His head was tilted back, and his mouth was open. He was snoring loudly.

"Well, whaddya know? What's he doing outside? The door was locked!" she exclaimed, puzzled. She shook him lightly and then harder. He ended up opening his eyes, appalled. He sat up straight. "Did you sleep out here all night?"

He made a forced smile. "That's right, Mrs. Ricardo. I don't know how it happened. I came outside to smoke. I didn't want to disturb anyone. When I was about to go back in, the door was locked, I don't know why. I didn't want to wake you up."

She shook her head, mortified. "How did it happen? The children were in bed!"

"Maybe they decided to play a prank on me. You know what children are like."

"Oh no! They all know better than that. They would never do anything like this. Now go up to your room and rest. I'll sort this out when I get back!"

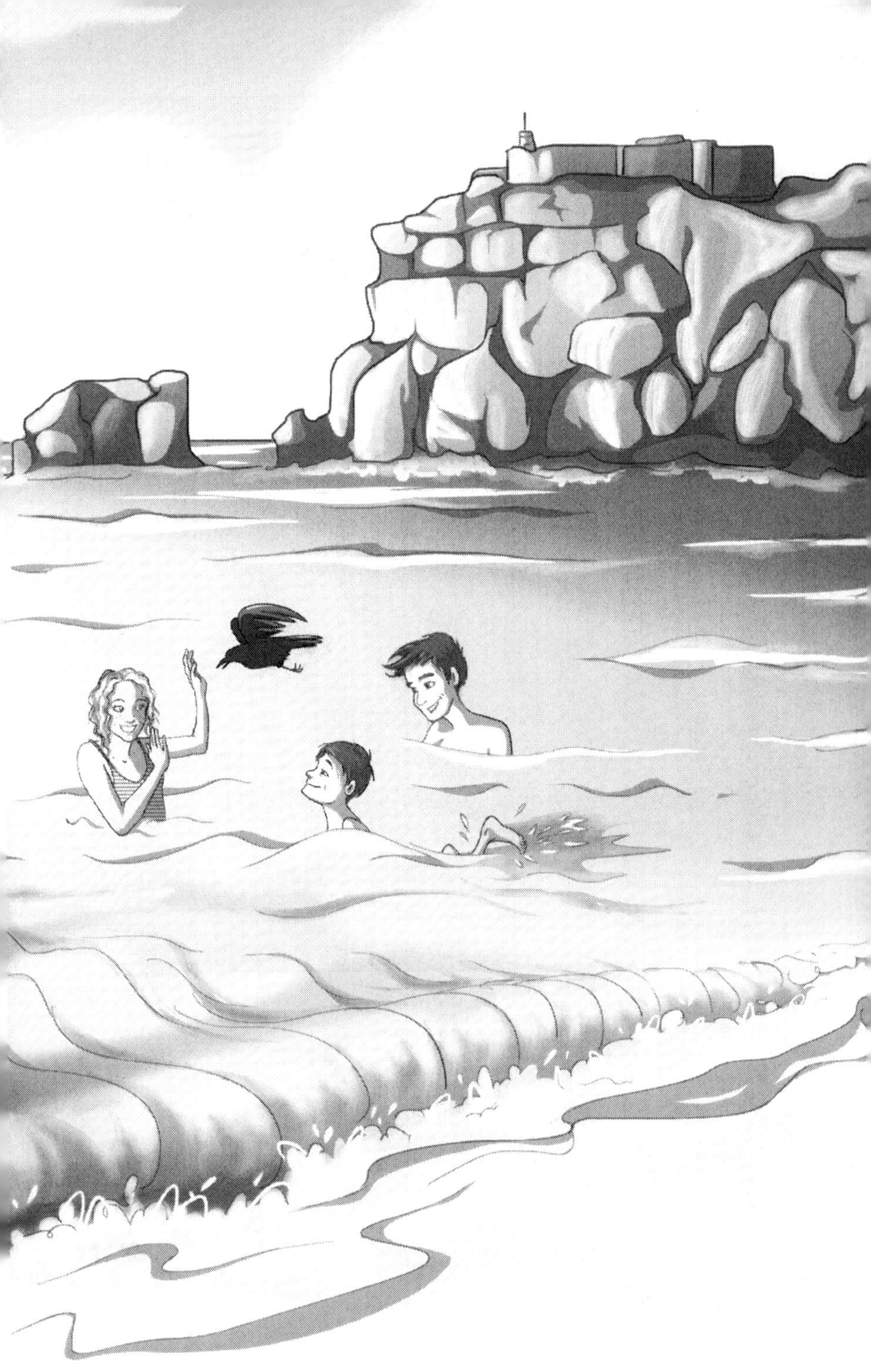

Chapter 6

An unpleasant argument

When the four children went downstairs to have breakfast, they were surprised to see the lodger sitting at the table with Christine, who seemed to be upset.

They greeted them and sat down, uneasy. Lodgers did not usually have any meals there: they would only use the room.

"Did you have a good night's sleep?"

Everyone looked at each other, realizing that the tone in which she spoke was different. She looked suspicious.

«Hel-lo! Hel-lo! Well, whaddya know? RASCAL! NAUGHTY BOY!» Jack said, shouting the last words and startling Mr. Gomes. The crow burst out laughing, cocking his head to look at him.

Mr. Gomes was convinced the crow was making fun of him, even though he knew it was not possible. He pursed his lips so much they almost disappeared, which made him look threatening for a few seconds. Then he forced himself to smile.

Daniel looked at him out of the corner of his eye. He had a feeling he knew why the lodger had sat at the table with them. Now, in broad daylight, his idea did not seem so good anymore. He was afraid he might be punished again. Sleeping outside all night wasn't pleasant at all, he thought.

"Which of you locked Mr. Gomes outside?"

Tony, Chris and Bea looked at her as if they thought she had gone mad. They looked at each other, puzzled.

"What do you mean, Mom?"

Mr. Gomes cleared his throat. The crow did the same, delighted with his new skill. The man frowned. He hated that annoying bird so much!

"Well, one of you played a little prank on me yesterday. I went outside to smoke around midnight. When I tried to get back inside, someone had locked the door."

Daniel wrinkled his brow. He was irritated by Mr. Gomes's lies. He knew he had gone out much later. He wasn't smoking, as he had said, either. His mother wouldn't believe him, of course. Adults usually believed what adults said more often than they did children. He was nothing but a plain liar! He bit his lip, furious.

His cousin looked at him sideways. She had a feeling he did it. She felt sorry for the boy. Being stuck with cousins he had never met and didn't like was no picnic. Especially being punished for something one of them had done. He was certainly in for a much harder punishment now.

She put on her most captivating, naive look and looked down, pretending to be embarrassed. She surprised everyone by what she said—especially Daniel.

"OH! How awful! You were outside? Oh, Auntie, please believe me! I didn't mean it! I came down to the kitchen to have some water and I saw the door wasn't locked. I looked out, but I didn't see anyone. I thought you had forgotten to lock the door. I was afraid there might be thieves, so I locked it. I'm so sorry, Mr. Gomes! I really didn't mean it!" she confessed, eyes wide open.

Though Mr. Gomes forced himself to smile, he did not fool anyone. It was clear he was trying hard to hold back his irritation. Deep down, he must have been yearning to slap her.

"Why did you go outside to smoke, Mr. Gomes?" asked Daniel.

"I'm not sure I understand."

"Your room has a window. You could have smoked there."

Mr. Gomes laughed and patted his head. The boy was very displeased. He thought he was too old for that.

"You're right. The truth is I didn't remember there was one."

«Liar!» he thought, gritting his teeth. He didn't like him at all.

Christine looked at her niece and her younger son. Although she suspected something, she said nothing. If Bea had decided to take the blame to save her cousin from imminent punishment, it was not for her to interfere. Perhaps the situation might bring the four closer together. Who knew?

They went out into the garden after breakfast.

"That guy is a world-class cheat! He didn't go outside to smoke, and it was after one o'clock!" Daniel exclaimed angrily. "He was on his cell phone and his words were very suspicious. I don't like him at all! He's a fake and treacherous! By the way, thank you for taking the blame for me, Beat... Bea. It was really cool. I'm also sorry for all the nonsense I said yesterday. I don't even know why I said that. That's not what I think."

His cousin shifted, uncomfortable. His thanks and his apology were embarrassing for both.

"It was also my fault. I'm sorry, too."

The other two smiled.

They talked about the same topic for a few more minutes, laughing out loud when Daniel told them everything that had happened during the night. Everything seemed funnier when he told it. Then Christine called them. The crow, which had been laughing louder than any of them during the conversation, mimicked her.

They went back inside. Daniel pulled his brother back.

"Thanks for the pudding. It was great!"

Tony looked at him, puzzled.

"I didn't take you any pudding! I thought about it, but Mom must have guessed it and forbade me to do it."

"What? If it wasn't you, then who was it?"

"I don't know."

Their mother appeared at the door and called them.

"Do you want to go to the beach or what? The bus will be here soon. Otherwise, you'll have to walk or go on your bikes. It's a long way away, mind you," she said.

"We didn't bring any beach towels, Aunt Christine. It was all so sudden. Dad gave us money to buy them, though," said Bea, who loved the beach.

"You don't need to. You can take mine and Uncle's. They're brand new."

"Just get a towel for my sister, Aunt Christine. I'm not going. I don't like the beach."

Aunt Christine looked at him, surprised. "You don't like the beach?!"

"No. I never did. Too many people, sand everywhere. I hate to mingle with so many people. Besides, my skin's too white. Just a bit of sunshine and I peel away, unlike Bea. No matter how much sun she gets, she never gets that way," he said, a little annoyed at his aunt's insistence. "Also, I want to finish reading a book I brought along. I enjoy it a lot more. Don't worry about me, Aunt Christine. I'll be fine. I seldom go to the beach."

"Well, if that's what you want," she said, shrugging, still perplexed. When she saw her children looked like they were about to make some malicious remark, she looked at them in a way they knew all too well.

They immediately shut their mouths and did not utter a word, even though they felt a strong desire to do so.

"Make sure you're back home by lunchtime!"

Bea looked at her brother, annoyed. She knew what her cousins must have been thinking of him. Deep down, they were right. Sometimes it seemed he felt he was better than anyone else.

The three ran towards the bus stop a few minutes later. Jack was flying beside them. He landed on his owner's shoulder when he saw they were going to get on the bus. The first thing he did as soon as he entered was to greet everyone politely, which made everybody laugh, especially the driver, a smiling blue-eyed old man that the two brothers knew and with whom they got along.

They had a wonderful morning. The water was warm, the sun was hot and there were lots of people around. The boys were pleasantly surprised. Their cousin turned out to be an excellent companion.

She liked the sea as much as they did and stayed in the water longer than she was in the sand. She caught waves as well as they did and swam with all the right movements, unlike Daniel, who splashed all over the place. They entered the water a dozen times, laughing and playing. It seemed like they had known each other forever.

Jack didn't like the boys' strange love of water. He wanted to land on the girl's shoulder, but much to his disappointment, she spent most of the time in the water like the other two. He called them names repeatedly out of boredom, amusing everyone in the process.

Chris didn't have as much fun as he expected. He couldn't concentrate on the book. He kept thinking about the others, wondering if they were having fun.

He ended up getting up and leaving the room, taking his book downstairs, where he could hear his aunt vacuuming. She looked up when she saw him, noticing his annoyance. She unplugged the vacuum cleaner and stored it.

"Are you bored, Chris?"

"A little bit, Aunt Christine. Time goes by so slowly."

"I'm going to iron some clothes. If you want, you can keep me company. Feel free to read. I won't mind."

Chris accepted the suggestion. He sat down on a chair, trying to focus on his book. He looked up at his aunt every once in a while. She seemed lost in her thoughts and did not even notice the scorching heat.

After some time, he saw her storing the iron and take the freshly ironed clothes. To his great astonishment, she put them in the washing machine piece by piece, looking very intent on what she was doing. He looked at her, gaping, puzzled. Why would she wash the clothes she had just ironed?! How uncanny!

Aunt Christine switched on the washing machine. For a moment she just stared at the clothes going round and round. As she turned, she saw the boy staring at her.

"What is it? What did I do?"

"You're washing the clothes you had just ironed," he said, embarrassed.

She looked at him, mortified. "Oh! Oh, God! I did it again! Why does my mind work like this? Why am I like this? After all that work!"

They looked at each other and burst out laughing. Deep down, there was a funny side to the situation.

The three children returned sometime later. Chris heard their voices in his bedroom and tried to look happy, so they wouldn't find out how bored he had been in their absence.

"Make sure you wipe your feet! I don't want sand inside. I spent all morning vacuuming. How many times did you enter the water?" asked their mother, smiling at their happy faces.

«Wipe your feet! Naughty boy! Hel-lo!» said Jack, flying towards her and landing on her shoulder.

"Silly boy!" Aunt Christine laughed, proud that the bird liked her.

«Silly boy! Silly boy! Silly boy!»

"The water was awesome, Mom!"

"We entered the water more than twenty times."

"That many, huh?"

The three laughed happily.

"Now go upstairs and take a quick shower. Lunch is almost ready. Off you go!"

They ran up the stairs, leaving the towels by the kitchen door. Daniel was the first to get upstairs. He went into one of the bathrooms.

Bea went to the room she shared with her brother and smiled at him. "So, tell me. Aren't you sorry you didn't go to the beach with us? The water was wonderful!"

"Why should I regret it? You know I don't like the beach," Chris said, annoyed by the look of satisfaction on her face. "I had a much better time here."

She frowned, annoyed by the tone with which he had spoken to her. "It wouldn't hurt you to be nice to people—like Tony is nice to Daniel. You never give in, do you? Tony is nothing like that. He's really cool! I can see why Daniel is crazy about his brother! I wish you were more like him."

The boy blushed, angry. "Well, I'm glad I'm not. They may be nice, but they are rude."

"At least you could have been kind enough to go, if only to keep me company. That's what you should have done if you were a cool brother, so that I wouldn't feel alone."

"I don't think you missed me that much. You're the best of friends now. You'll be speaking like them anytime soon!"

"Oh! You're so kind! What's wrong with the way they speak? I think it's cute! They probably don't like the way we speak either. They must think we're stuck-up!"

"Come, now! It's not our fault that we're used to a different lifestyle. Mom and Dad would never let strangers stay in our house. It's a matter of education and culture!"

Suddenly, they stopped arguing. They realized they were not alone. Their cousins were by the bedroom door, looking very pale. They had heard most of the argument.

Chris and Bea looked at them in embarrassment.

"You think you're better than us. Well, you're wrong! You just think you're better than us, that's all! As for renting the rooms, we do it because we need the money, not because we like it. Dad's not a captain on a ship, like your Dad. We may be rude and not speak properly, but we'd never look down on someone who gave us a room to sleep in, even though we didn't know they could be making money from that same room to help pay the mortgage!" Tony said in a single breath. "If you think you're so much better than us, why didn't you go to a hotel?!"

There was an unpleasant silence.

Christine appeared by the door. She could see they had been arguing.

"Are you all deaf? Didn't you hear me calling for lunch? Godmom called to invite you to come and help her move. Do you want to go?"

They nodded in embarrassment.

"I thought so. I told her you were going. She'll drop by after lunch to leave Agnes. She'd only get in the way. She'd put back out everything you'd put in—plus she'd keep nagging the removals men with tons of questions," she said, smiling, delighted at the thought of having her niece's company for the rest of the day. She thought the little girl was very funny and she had a lot of fun with her cleverness.

Christine watched them go down the stairs, thinking. When would all the arguments between them end? They were too different from each other to get along.

Her sister had thought they would eventually get along and perhaps learn something useful from each other. She doubted it. She did not see any great improvement in the relationship between the four cousins. Perhaps they would find something in common that would bring them together. She had no idea what it might be.

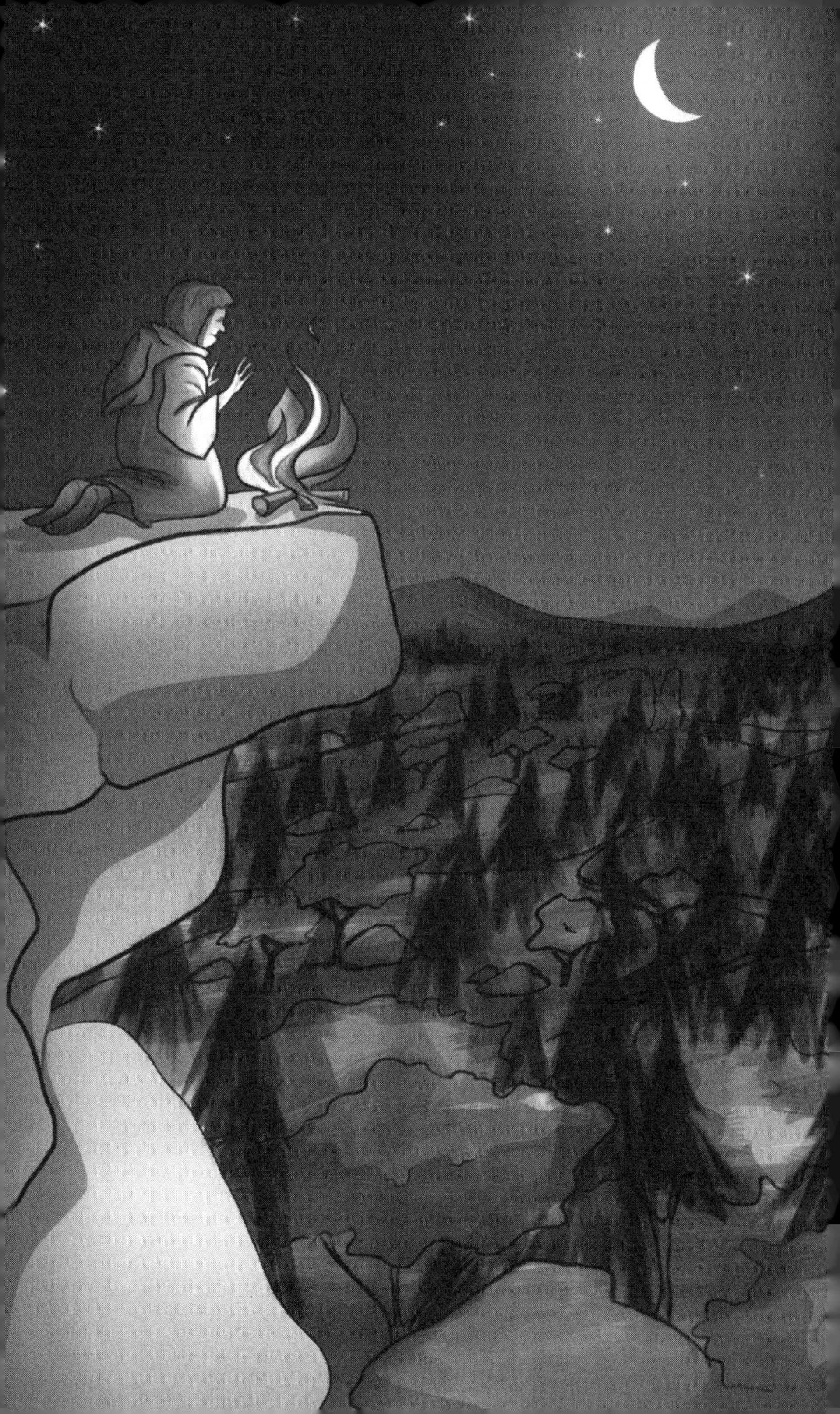

Chapter 7

A very interesting discovery

After lunch, the children's aunt and godmother dropped by and left her daughter. She kept talking to them during the drive towards her house. She was as excited as a child who had a new toy. She ended up making them laugh and get in a better mood and forget the nasty argument they had had hours before.

At home were now Christine, little Agnes and the lodger, who was a bit relieved to see them leave. He needed to search their rooms and, if possible, get some information from Christine. As he was opening the last drawer in Bea and Chris's room's dresser, a cheerful little voice behind him made him jump.

"What are you doing?" The little girl was holding a doll. She looked him up and down.

He forced himself to smile. "Oh! Hello, little girl. Who are you? What's your doll's name?"

"I'm Agnes. My baby's named is Joel. He's very cute. What are you doing?"

He frowned. She hadn't forgotten what she had asked him first. He put his index finger over his lips. "It's a secret."

"Oh!"

She ran out. Balthazar, who was afraid she might tell her aunt and put him in a slightly awkward position, followed her.

"She's so smart, Mrs. Ricardo! She talks so much, too! That's not very common in such a small child, is it? I have a nephew who's two. He only says a couple of words."

Christine looked away from the lace on the sheet she was ironing. Agnes was looking him up and down intently, holding the doll against her chest.

"That's right. She began to speak at a very early age. You can keep a conversation with her, too. You're never lonely when she's around!"

"Does your sister have any other children?"

"She also has a seven-year-old boy. He's very smart, too. You know, my sister is a writer. I'm the reason why she began to read," she said, smiling proudly. "She gets along very well with the children. In fact, she's Daniel and Beatrix's godmother. The other two call her Zaza and Zazabeth ever since they learned how to speak."

"Oh, do they?" he said, pretending to be interested. He wanted to get to know more about the other children, but he didn't know how to begin. "So, the other kids are your brother's children?"

"No. I only have one sister. They're my cousin's children. We were raised together. It's as if we were brother and sister. His children call me Aunt."

"Oh, do they? What does your cousin do for a living?"

The little girl came near him, looking very serious. "What's your name?"

He smiled, trying to win her sympathy. "My name's Balthazar. What's yours?"

"I told you upstairs."

Gomes was startled.

Christine didn't notice anything. She was focused on the clothes she was ironing.

"So you did! You're absolutely right. You're Agnes."

"Yes, I am. And my baby's name is Joel."

"Michael is the captain of a passenger ship. We don't see each other a lot. He's more attached to my sister. They are really close, despite the age difference. I'm sure if he had any secrets, he would trust her to keep them. The same goes for her."

"How interesting!" he remarked. His eyes were shining in a strange way.

"You're bald! My baby's bald, too!" Agnes said with a mischievous laugh. She was staring at his bald spot, feeling a great urge to pat him the way she used to pat her doll.

He shuddered. He had forgotten about her. He blinked, flustered. He tried to smile but failed to do so.

Christine bit her lip to keep herself from laughing and turned her face to the side. He noticed it. The girl was such a pest! She kept talking and talking. He felt like gagging her and slapping her.

Just when he was about to ask another question, the girl made another remark. He was dumbfounded.

"You have a huuuuge nose!"

Christine barely managed not to laugh. She coughed instead, to disguise it. "You mustn't say things like that, Agnes. Mr. Gomes may not like it!"

The little girl stared at her with wide eyes.

"It's true! He does, yeah!"

"Never mind, Mrs. Ricardo. I know how children are like. Does your sister live nearby?"

Much to his despair, she didn't stop talking.

"My little baby's forehead hurts so much. He's sooooo sick! I must take him to the hospital. The doctor will give him a shot. Poor little thing! He has a fever," she said, taking the doll's hat off, wrapping it up and placing it on the doll's forehead, as if it were a compress. Do you like having shots? I don't like it at all. It really hurts!"

"You're so funny, Agnes. Why don't you go lay your baby on his crib?" he suggested. He was exasperated.

"Oh, he's much better, now!"

"Where did you say your sister lives, Mrs. Ricardo?"

She took some clothes, went into the dining room, and answered. "Near the harbor. In the old ranger's house."

The man smiled triumphantly. Suddenly, he noticed the girl was staring at him.

"You have *sooooo* many teeth!"

He wanted to answer that it was all the better to eat her, like the Big Bad Wolf, but he stopped himself from doing so. Smart as she was, she might answer back. Taking advantage of her aunt's absence, he took the doll from her and lifted it out of her reach, smiling mockingly.

"The baby's mine! Give me my baby! Give it to me now! Now!"

Gomes grimaced, vindictive. He hated children. "Your baby is very ugly."

She frowned, indignant, and kicked him in the shin.

"No, he isn't! Joel is beautiful and cuddly, and you are *sooooo* ugly!" she shouted. She punched him in a slightly "delicate" place as hard as she could.

Gomes dropped the doll on the floor, bending over in pain.

"Did you hurt yourself, Joel? Did you?" Agnes asked, taking it in her arms, worried. She looked up at the man, angry. "Go away! You're mean!"

She hit him right in his shin once more and left, holding her nose up high.

"Jesus! She's worse than the rest of them! I'd smack you so much if I could, you pest!" he mumbled.

He ended up giving up on the questioning and went outside. He was determined to find out where the ranger's house was.

Meanwhile, the children were having a good time carrying boxes and crates, excited. The little boy was the most excited of all. He wouldn't stand still or silent until his mother warned him, exasperated.

"Do you see that fig tree, Andy? If you don't stop it now, I'll tie you to it until we're done. And if you think I'm kidding, you're wrong."

Her son gave her a wide-eyed look and burst out laughing, which made her laugh, too. He calmed down for a few minutes, but soon started again. His mother eventually sent him outside, together with the crow, who kept telling everyone to wipe their feet. They could no longer stand him. And so Jack found himself shooed away by his owner as if he were a chicken. He let out an indignant scream.

The house didn't look the same anymore. It was surrounded by a beautiful white wooden fence. The walls were pink and had white shutters. There were red swings and a slide of the same color in the back. The garden had already been tended to and promised to become beautiful.

Inside, the house was painted white. Although the rooms were much smaller than the ones in two boys' home, everything looked nice. The kitchen was the largest room in the house. The furniture was already there, even though everything was still a mess.

The owner of the house was busy arranging clothes and dishes, hanging curtains, making beds. She had instructed the four of them to dust the books and put them on the shelves. There were many books.

"What's this little book?" murmured Chris, more to himself than to the others. He leafed through it and his interest gradually increased. "Come and have a look! This book is about the history of Nazaré. It looks very old. There are pirates and a monk who took shelter in the cliff. There are caves, too."

The others looked at each other, thrilled. "Caves?"

"Yeah. Let's ask Zazabeth. Maybe she knows something about it!"

They all ran to the room where they knew she was and rushed in.

"Hi! Don't tell me you've finished unpacking all the books," she said, smiling. She noticed the book Chris was holding. "Oh! You found it."

"Is it true what's written here, Zaza? Were there pirates around here?"

"Yes, there were. But no one lived down here yet—only fishermen. Back then people lived in Pederneira. It's all there, I think. There's also a very interesting story about King Rodrigo and Friar Romano. King Rodrigo hid in Monte de São Brás, the hill just outside Nazaré, next to the Orbitur camping site. Friar Romano lived up the hill at Sítio. They'd build a fire every night to find out how they were both doing."

"That's so exciting, Godmom!" Bea exclaimed, her eyes shining.

"I thought the same when I found that book. It's very old. I don't even remember how I got it. It was written by a priest. I was so excited I couldn't think of anything else. I began to think there were caves under the cliff because of what the priest says in the book, also because of something I discovered, and for the stories my Grandmother used to tell."

"What did you discover, Godmom?" asked Daniel excitedly. He couldn't be still.

She sat on the edge of the bed, her eyes shining with excitement. Meanwhile, the children sat on the carpet, as silent as mice.

"An amazing discovery, or so it seemed to me at the time. I'll tell you all about in a moment. The book tells the story of the Image of Our Lady of Nazaré, from the time it was sculpted by St Joseph until it reached these parts. Legend has it that the Image of Our Lady of Nazareth was given as an offer to a convent in Spain, where it was revered by the monks and the people. In 714, the Moors invaded the Iberian Peninsula. The King of the Goths, King Rodrigo, was defeated. He ran away disguised as a shepherd. A long time later, he got to the monastery I told you about. He knelt before the only image he found there and passed out. He was exhausted. The monks had already left the convent carrying everything they could and taken refuge inside the walls of Merida, as they feared for their lives. Only one had remained: Friar Romano."

"That's very interesting, Godmom, but you still haven't told us what you discovered!" Daniel remarked anxiously. His brother nudged him.

"I'll get to that. Don't be impatient. This will help you better understand the rest. Moving on. King Rodrigo ended up telling the monk who he really was. They decided to flee from the invaders towards the West, carrying the small image and a vault with relics given to the monastery by St Augustine. On November, 22, they saw the sea. They had reached the outskirts of what would become Nazaré. Fearing the Moors, they climbed a hill, which we now call Monte de São Brás, which is hard to access, full of brush and rocks. There they found a deserted chapel with a large crucifix and a grave."

"So they hid there," Bea said, wide-eyed. She seemed to be picturing the whole scene: the two tired men going up the hill and making this discovery in such a deserted place.

"They did, for some time. They fed on herbs, roots, and wild berries. But Friar Romano was an old man. It was getting harder for him to climb the hill. He ended up moving to the cliff that could be seen from there, Sítio. He built an altar for the Image between two steep rocks over the sea and he dug a cave for himself."

"So they never saw each other again?"

"No, Tony. They had agreed to light a fire at the top of the hill and the cliff every night to know that they were both well. If you go to Sítio, you'll find you can see Monte de São Brás perfectly."

"Then what happened?" asked Chris, interested.

"One night, Friar Romano didn't answer back. King Rodrigo set out, worried about his fate. When he got there, he found him dead. He buried him at the feet of the Image of Our Lady and left. He never returned there, disheartened by the death of his friend. He too died sometime later."

"What about the vault with the relics?" asked Daniel, yearning with curiosity, imagining a vault full of gold and precious stones.

"It was also hidden in the cave. The Image remained there for four centuries—Sítio was a desolate place in those days. It was found by shepherds as late as 1179. It was that very same Image that, according to legend, the Mayor of Porto de Mós, Dom Fuas Roupinho, found years later," she continued, after a quick pause. "And so, the famous Miracle of Our Lady of Nazaré happened. That's how the place where the Image was found got its name: Sítio[1]. Dom Fuas Roupinho ordered the building of a chapel, which became known as the Chapel of Memory. When the altar was demolished to build the chapel, the vault containing the relics was found, as well as a parchment telling the story of the Image and why it had come to Nazaré."

"But—what about the vault? Where is it?"

Their godmother laughed at his enthusiasm and resumed the narrative.

---

1. Legend has it that Dom Fuas Roupinho chased a deer to the top of a cliff on a foggy morning in 1182. The deer fell off, but his horse miraculously stopped at the very edge of that place (*sítio*, in Portuguese).

"I don't know. They never mention it again. I have no idea what happened to it."

"What about the cave?"

"When Dom Fuas had the altar demolished to build the chapel in 1182, the cave was buried."

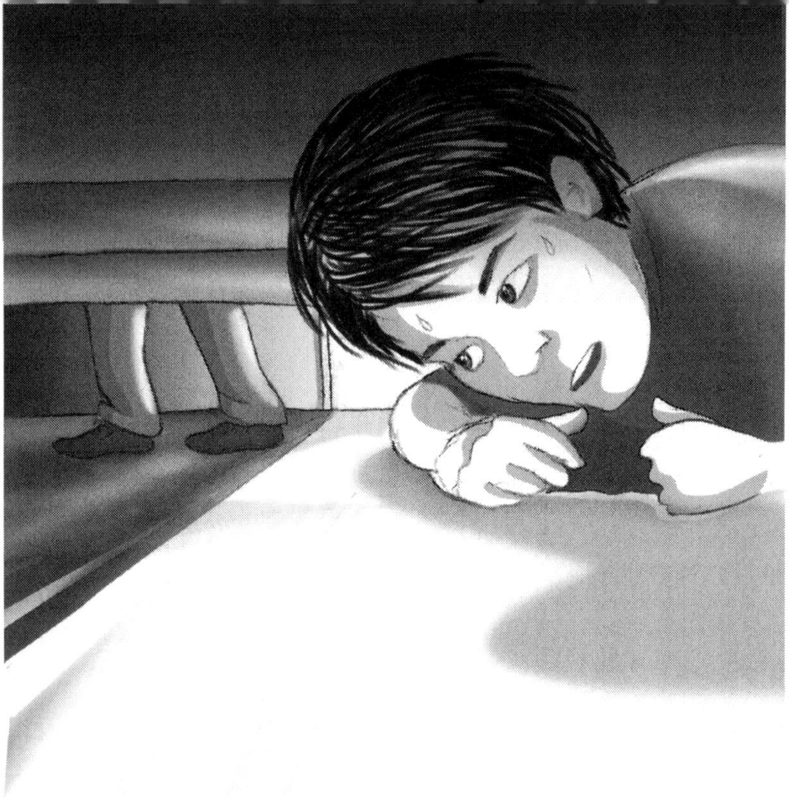
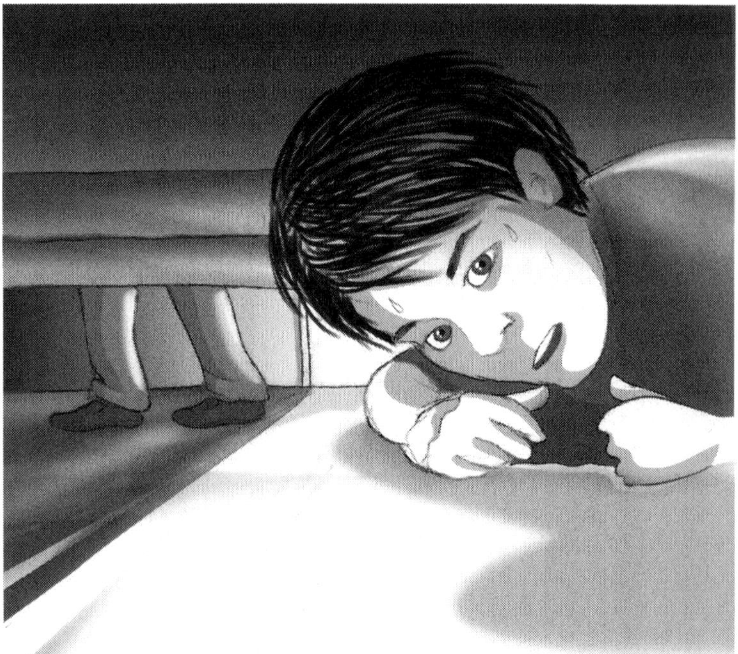

Chapter 8

Fascinating stories

It felt like a cold-water bucket had been dumped on them. They could see themselves exploring Friar Romano's cave. They looked at her with disappointment on their faces.

"Buried!?"

"Yes, but in 1585, another monk, Brother Bernardo de Brito from the Monastery of Alcobaça, who had been appointed chronicler of the Kingdom and was very learned, discovered in the monastery archive the donation of land made to Our Lady of Nazaré by Dom Fuas Roupinho, as well as the parchment he had found in Friar Romano's cave. Some years later, in 1600, he decided to unblock the cave with the help of a few devotees. He left a wooden copy of the Image at the entrance to the cave."

"A copy? Why?"

"The original chapel was made up of four open arches, so that the Image could be seen from land and sea. As the years went by, the Image became damaged due to the salt air and the wind. So, in 1370, King Fernando I ordered the closing of the chapel arches and, years later, the construction of a grand temple (the one that now stands on the square in front of the church) and moved the Image there to protect it," she said, her eyes shining with enthusiasm. "I read the whole book. The inscriptions left by Friar Bernardo de Brito on the tiles of the Chapel of Memory, which you can see in the book, read that the great crucifix found by Friar Romano and King Rodrigo in the chapel at Monte de São Brás is the same one that is in the sacristy. As I was full of curiosity, I went to Sítio. There's a life-sized cross with Jesus nailed to it in the sacristy. The crucifix stands on a large black stone. You must really look for it to see it, because it's behind a glass box with Baby Jesus inside, a kind of alms box. I took a closer look at it and I noticed the stone is a sort of map of the place where the Chapel of Memory was built. It's full of underground caves. That's where Friar Romano is buried."

"The children looked at each other. Their faces were flushed, and their eyes were shining. They were so excited they could hardly speak. Eventually they pinched each other. For the first time, they were united by a common feeling. Oh, how they'd like to find those caves! What if they managed to find them?!

"Has anyone discovered them?" Bea inquired, anxiously.

"Well, there are some stories about it. You'd better ask your great-grandmother. In fact, it was because of the stories she told me that I became convinced that there must be caves all over the place under the cliff."

"We must talk to Great-Grandma, Zaza!" Tony decided, getting up so suddenly he toppled his cousin.

Zaza laughed when she saw their faces full of hope.

"Well. I think I can take a break. Come on! I'll take you to Grandma! You better call Andy and Jack."

They ran outside and squeezed in to fit in the car. They had a hard time finding a parking spot: the place was packed with tourists. Finally, they managed to park and set out.

Their great-grandmother lived with Chris and Bea's grandmother in a street everyone called Augusta, though it had an entirely different name.

They burst into the house, talking. The crow was making more noise than all of them put together. Even though she was

98, their great-grandmother was still sharp. She was very thin and a little stooped. She looked smart and nice. She had just one tooth left in her lower jaw. She wore traditional local clothes, but they were black, as she had been a widow for many years. She smiled, delighted at the sight of her granddaughter and her five great-grandchildren, who kissed her.

"I'd like you to tell them those stories from back when I was a little girl, Grandma. The one about the cave under the lighthouse and the cave of Our Lady of Nazaré. Do you remember them?"

The old lady looked satisfied. She loved to talk about the old days. She remembered events that had happened ages ago better than recent ones. She knew stories about beings from another world that would make your hair stand on end.

The children sat at her feet, excited.

"When I was a girl, the beach didn't look as it does today. It was bigger and the sea, as it were, began where the lighthouse stands. When the tide was low, we used to walk between Pedra do Guilhim and the *suberco* to go to the beach at Praia do Norte. I remember carts going by there as if it were today. I took that same path many times, too," she told them. Her eyes were shining, longing for the time when she was a girl.

The children opened their eyes wide in amazement. They pictured loaded carts and people passing by where now there was only water, the sea kissing their bare feet. They were almost in a trance, enchanted by the old lady's words, envying her for having been there in those days. They knew the people from Nazaré call the cliff *suberco*, so they were not surprised.

"It wasn't always like this. Many centuries ago, the sea used to flood all of Nazaré, Valado dos Frades and even Fervença and Maiorga, which are a few miles away on the way to Alcobaça. Monte de São Brás, which was called Seano back then, was surrounded by the sea," added her granddaughter, her eyes shining brightly. The four cousins' faces reminded her of what she had felt when her grandmother told her those ancient stories about such distant times. "Little by little, the sea receded, and it was just like Grandma says. But now the sea has been claiming the beach."

Arminda, the children's great-grandmother, nodded.

"What your Godmother wants me to tell you is that, when we passed under the *suberco*, there was a cave and—lo and behold!—there was a long stone table and stone benches there. The old ones used to say that was where pirates used to meet. They called it Boca do Inferno. Nobody dared enter there."

"OH!!"

"For real?" asked Tony, wide-eyed with enthusiasm.

"Yes. I saw it myself."

Bea and Chris's grandmother sat on the sofa next to them, smiling.

"It's true. One day, when I was Andy's age, the tide went down a lot and I went there with your Grandmother," she told the other two.

"Godmom said you know some stories about the cave under the Chapel of Memory, too. Has anyone ever entered there?"

"There once was a shepherd who stepped into the hole looking for his dog that had run away from him. No one saw him again. There was another time when a priest also disappeared down there. He was never heard from again. It's true. The poor man was never seen again. People began to be afraid, so bars were put at the entrance to the cave so that no one could enter and meet their death there."

The children looked at each other, disappointed.

"So, you can't go in?"

Their great-grandmother looked at them, indignant. "Of course not! The priest is the only one who has the key. He will never give it to anyone. It's very dangerous!"

Those words were still in their minds when they headed for the car, a little sad after all the excitement. They could see themselves entering the cave, discovering another cave and then another, each cave more amazing than the previous one.

"I'm so disappointed, Godmom! I thought we'd be able to explore the cave. Can you imagine how exciting it would be?"

"I can, actually. I had the same idea when I was your age. I went to the chapel a few times, whenever I had a chance—you see, it's usually full of people. I kept thinking of a way to get inside, but I never found one. It was locked tight. It was so frustrating. The cave was right there, and I couldn't get in! I know how you're feeling right now."

"It probably leads to cave Great-Granma talked about," said Chris.

"Maybe. In that case, it would be useless. The cave is now under the sea. Besides, I always imagined there must be more than one cave. If you go to Praia do Norte, you'll notice the rocks are full of openings."

"Did you look there, too, Godmom?"

"Of course, Daniel. I was very adventurous—and stubborn, too. When something got into my head, nothing would ever get it out. Then, one day, my stubbornness was rewarded. At the end of the summer, I discovered a cave!"

The boys stopped, excited, making the people who were walking behind them bump into them.

"Tell us, Zaza! You must tell us! We have to know!"

"Okay,' she agreed, laughing. She opened the car door and they all sat down. "I went to Praia do Norte and found a hole. I went inside, but I saw little, as you can imagine. I bought a flashlight and went in again. There was a very deep hole on my right, and I could perfectly see very white sand. In front of me, further to the left, there was a kind of path that went up and curved towards Sítio. I climbed a little, but it was difficult to walk on the rocks unaided. Then I was afraid the tide might go up and I'd be trapped there. I went out just in time. The tide was already over the opening. I had to wait between two waves to go outside on the beach."

The five children were staring at her. Their eyes were shining with excitement.

"So, it's still there!"

"I never saw it again—not even when the tide is low. As I told you, the sea has been rising every year. The opening must be covered by now for sure."

"OH!!"

"Don't be so disappointed. You can explore the entire cliff on the Praia do Norte side. There are many openings there. There's also a large roofless cave with a hole in the middle, which the old ones call Forno d'Orca— don't ask me why they call it the Orca's Oven. I went there a few times. It was always wet. There was water dripping—it looked good, so I thought there must be a spring inside the cliff. You may not know this, but on the other side—on the beach, that is—there's a fountain. They say the water is very good. It's probably the same one; it just flows along different paths."

"Cool!"

"Great!"

"Promise me, if you decide to go to Praia do Norte to explore the cliff, you won't set foot in the sea. It's very dangerous and bathing is not allowed there. Many good swimmers have drowned there."

"You can rest assured, Zaza. Nobody will get their feet wet. If we want to bathe, we'll go to the beach down here. We know well the gigantic waves that are formed there[2]!"

---

2. Nazaré is famous in the world of surfing for the gigantic waves that are formed in Praia do Norte, the North Beach. Garrett McNamara rode a 78-ft wave there on November 1, 2011, Rodrigo Koxa rode an 80-ft wave on November 8, 2017, and Maya Gabeira rode a 73.5-ft wave on February 11, 2020, breaking her own record, which she had set there as well. They have been listed in the Guinness World Records for the largest wave ever surfed (male, in the case of the former two, and female in the latter).

Soon they were back at the two boys' house. They were excited. They got together in their room to talk. They did not need to express what they were feeling in words. They were all thinking about the same: to discover the entrance to one of the caves!

"The first thing we need to do is buy flashlights!" said Tony, rubbing his hands excitedly.

Chris nodded. "Then we'll go to the Chapel of Memory to have a look at the entrance to the cave. We'll wait till no one is there and then we'll think about what we should do next."

"Right! Oh, we must also have a look at the crucifix in the sacristy!" Daniel reminded them. He was so excited he couldn't sit still. "Take Jack away from here, Bea! It looks like he wants to tear off my shoelaces."

"Stand still, naughty boy! Shouldn't we tell Godmom when we start investigating on our own? After all, it was she who told us about it," said Bea, patting the crow, who whispered something they didn't understand.

They looked at each other, doubtful. Tony shook his head, determined.

"Better not. Zaza may be cool, but she's an adult. She might forbid us if she knew we were going to venture into Praia do Norte."

"Still, because of what she told us, she must suspect we're going to do it."

"Okay, Bea. Anyway, she probably thinks we won't find anything. Remember she said she looked for the same entrance several times, but couldn't find again", Chris said, his blue eyes shining like stars. He gave the bird, who was busy pulling his shoelaces, a push.

«Naughty boy! Rascal! Well, whaddya know?»

They laughed, then looked at each other, embarrassed, remembering the arguments they had had.

They looked so silly now!

"We're sorry for what we said. We didn't mean to hurt you. The truth is we liked it as much as you did when Dad made us come here."

"Chris is right. We shouldn't have behaved like that. You had all the reasons to be more upset than we did," Bea agreed, smiling.

Daniel and Tony found themselves thinking that their cousin was pretty and nice after all, when she was not in a bad mood and looking stuck-up.

"Let's just forget about the whole thing. We didn't behave very well either."

They shook hands, serious. Then Bea exclaimed, amazed:

"Someone's been messing with my stuff! That drawer wasn't like that!"

Daniel jumped up, furious. "I hope you're not implying we've been messing with your stuff."

"Of course not, Daniel. Don't be so suspicious. Of course, it was neither of us, and neither was Mom."

They looked at each other.

They were thinking the same thing.

"It must have been that Balthazar Gomes!"

"What with all the news Zaza told us, we totally forgot to tell her what happened tonight!"

Suddenly, they saw the two younger boys looked surprised. Tony and Chris realized they had said too much. They decided to tell them everything, without leaving any detail out.

"Now, don't act strange whenever he's around. We mustn't let him think we suspect him."

"So, the rascal came looking in our room for whatever it was Dad sent Godmom. The nerve of him!" exclaimed Bea, indignant.

«Well, whaddya know? Rascal!»

"What if we did the same?"

"What do you mean, Daniel?"

"What if I search his room to see if we find anything?"

The others looked at each other, pleased with the idea.

They smiled, their eyes shining bright.

Daniel jumped up, dashed out of the room, and headed for the lodger's room. The others watched from the door. They saw him knock on the door. There was no answer, so he turned the handle slowly and went inside.

"One of us should keep a watch, in case the rascal returns and surprises Daniel," Tony said. "We'll take turns."

Daniel started to open the closet doors as soon as he got in the room. He didn't find anything there, neither on the dresser nor on the nightstand. He stood still in the middle of the room, disconcerted. That's weird! Nobody goes away on vacation without bringing at least a comb and a pair of socks—unless he had suddenly decided to travel. That must be it! As he was about to leave the room, Daniel realized the handle was turning. He heard voices coming from the other side of the door: the lodger and Bea's voices. He took a quick look around, trying to find a place to hide. He mustn't find him there!

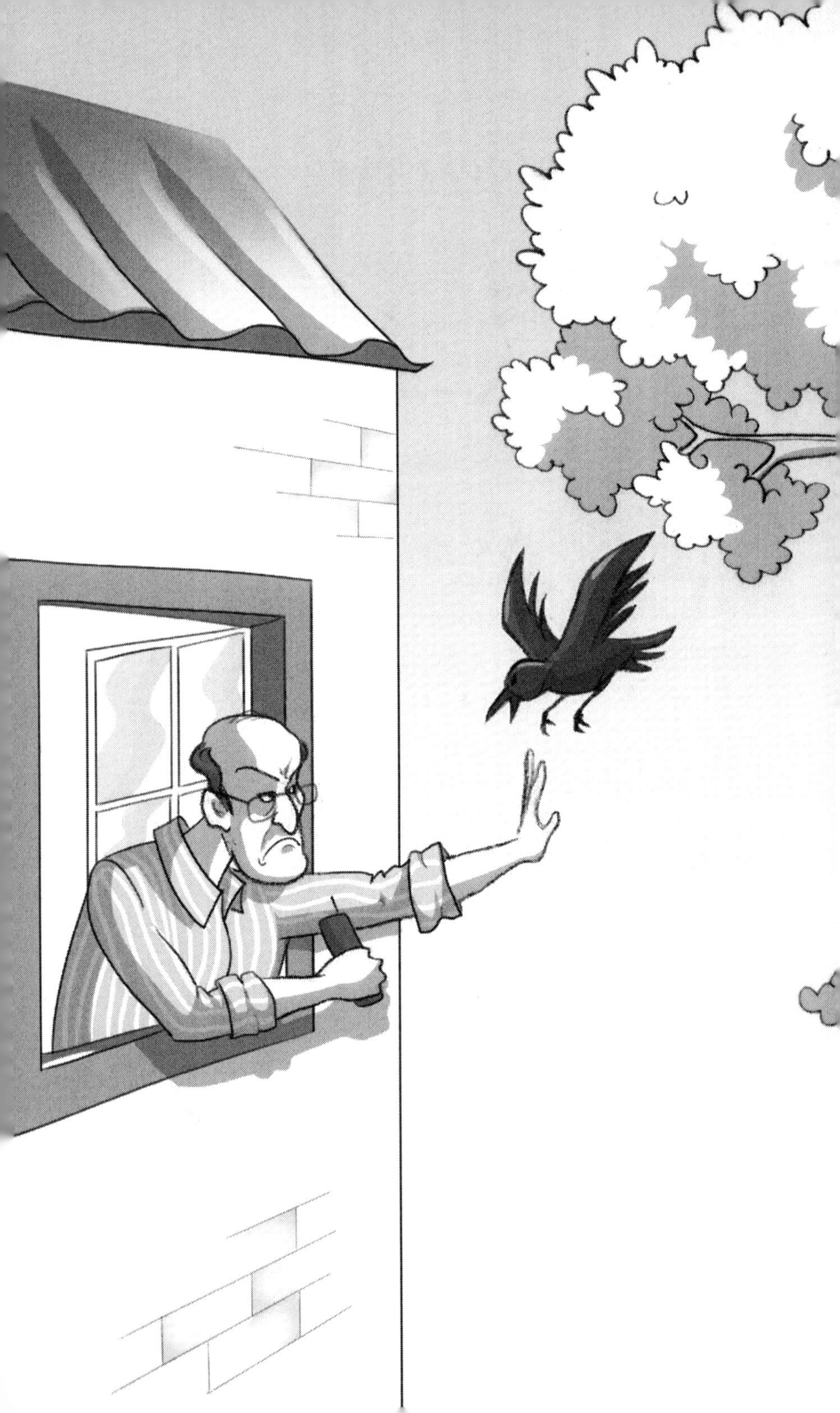

Chapter 9

Jack has a great time!

Daniel's heart nearly jumped out of his mouth when he saw Mr. Gomes enter the room. He could only see his legs, for he had hidden under the bed. He heard him mumble under his breath and cringed when he realized he was about to sit on the bed. Rats! He didn't see that coming. Now he couldn't leave without being seen.

In the other room, the three children were trying hard to think of a way to get him out. Eventually, it was Jack who solved the problem, even though he wasn't aware of it, of course. Jack saw the window was open, so he flew out and landed on a tree. He had fun hopping from one tree branch to another. Then he spotted the neighbor's cat sleeping next to the wall that separated the two houses. Jack knew from experience that cats were terrified when they heard him barking, so he did his best impersonation of a furious dog.

The cat jumped up, startled, when it heard barking right next to him. It fell to the ground on all fours, snorting, scared, arching its body. It looked around, but there was no dog in sight.

Suddenly, Jack took flight and barked right next to it. The cat jumped up even higher. It snorted at the crow, disconcerted, and raised its paw threateningly.

«Well, whaddya know? You fool!»

The perfect impersonation of its terrified meow made the cat dash towards its owners' house. A bird meowing and barking like its archenemies! *The horror!* the cat probably thought.

Jack paced the wall, annoyed. There was no one else around to frighten. When he raised his head, he saw Mr. Gomes holding his cell phone near an open window. The crow remembered he didn't like him and flew towards him.

«Rascal! You naughty boy!» he said, mimicking Christine's voice.

Gomes looked around, surprised, but did not see the bird. He continued to speak softly. A few seconds later, he heard the same words, this time in his own voice. He was speechless. So was the person he was talking to.

«Why did you call me rascal and a naughty boy?» asked an irritated voice on the phone.

Gomes looked around suspiciously. As soon as he peeked out, he was pecked on the face. He automatically touched where it hurt with the hand that wasn't holding the cell phone. There was blood on it. He tried to grab the crow and stretched so much out the window he nearly fell. Jack flew away, laughing out loud despondently.

"Damn it! I'll twist your neck when I get you, you idiot! All I need is to catch you off guard!" he grunted in a low voice.

He came close to the mirror and shuddered when he saw the wound. A tuft of his beard was gone. He looked strange now. First, he was red with anger, then turned to a beautiful shade of purple. He used a handkerchief to stop the blood from running down his face.

An increasingly irritated voice could be heard on the cell phone, insulting him.

"Take it easy, Cruz! I wasn't talking to you! The damned bird did it again! He took off a bit of my beard and my face, the rascal! I'll kill him when this is all over, just as sure as my name is Bernard Nunes!"

Daniel had to stop himself from bursting out laughing, to the point of not feeling well. The situation couldn't be funnier.

The fake Balthazar Gomes ended the call and left, heading for the bathroom in search of a way to clean his wound.

Daniel got up as soon as he saw him leave. He went to the door and carefully peered out into the hall. Then he ran towards the room where the others were and threw himself on the bed, laughing out loud. He couldn't hold it any longer. Tears were streaming down his face as he recalled everything that had happened.

His brother and his cousins were looking at him, puzzled. They had no idea why he was laughing himself silly.

The crow appeared by the window and jumped up to its owner's shoulder. Jack seemed a bit overwhelmed. He knew all too well he shouldn't peck people. Still, he couldn't help it. He just couldn't understand why that man would wear so much hair on his face instead of wearing it on his head.

Daniel laughed even more when he saw him. The bird mimicked his laughter, much to his delight.

"You won't believe what that rascal did! He's really smart! It's as if he realized I was in trouble! What a cool bird!"

Bea smiled. She was pleased to hear her friend's compliments. When she learned about everything that had happened, she laughed her head off, just like the others.

"Way to go, Jack!" Tony praised him as he patted him.

The others did the same. The crow was happy: he loved being patted.

"I hope he won't say anything to Aunt Christine," Chris suddenly remembered.

Everyone was silent for a moment. They hoped from the bottom of their hearts that would not happen. She'd be very angry. Who knows? She might end up locking up Jack in a cage. Bea winced at the thought of it.

"Did you find anything in his room?" Bea asked softly.

"Not a thing. Strange, isn't it? There was nothing in the drawers. I did manage to hear some of the things he said on the phone. He said something about a CD several times. He mentioned you guys, too—and your Dad. Nobody seems to know where he is."

"So that's what Dad sent Zazabeth—a CD."

"What could be so important for Gomes to come after you?" asked Tony. "Isn't your Dad just the captain of a passenger ship?"

His cousins looked at each other, bewildered.

"We thought so. It looks like we were wrong."

"I wonder if Mom's aware of Dad's secret job," Bea said, staring at her brother.

"Of course she is. He would never hide anything like that from her. Zazabeth must know all about it, too."

This is so mysterious and exciting!"

"I wonder if your Dad is spying for the government," said Daniel. His eyes were shining with excitement. He was picturing him in big trouble, James Bond-style. He envied him. It would be great to lead such a fascinating life!

His cousins shrugged. This was all new to them.

Christine called them a little while later. They ran downstairs. They were starving.

As usual, their uncle was not at the table: he was away at sea. His nephews had only met him one morning when he had gotten up for lunch, but he left for the harbor after the meal was over.

Much to their amazement, the lodger was sitting at the table, too. They observed the round-shaped bandage on the left side of his face and tried hard not to laugh. The sight of the dish full of stuffed squid made them forget how unpleasant it was to sit in front of that ghastly creature. Christine smiled.

"Mr. Gomes brought these squid a while ago. Can you believe it? They're so fresh! You shouldn't have bothered, Mr. Gomes. Thank goodness there's always fresh fish at home. You needn't have spent so much money," said Aunt Christine, smiling.

The children looked at each other, realizing this was a way for him to impress her and get closer to the family, God knows why.

Mr. Gomes gave the crow a hateful look, which did not go unnoticed. Bea shivered. If looks could kill, Jack would have dropped dead at her feet.

"Take a seat. I'll serve you in no time. As for you, Mr. Jack, stop pecking bread!" she scolded him, smiling. She served the lodger and then her nephews and her children. "Mr. Gomes was about to tell me how he hurt his face."

He forced himself to smile.

"It seems your bird isn't very fond of me."

She looked at him, mortified.

"Oh, no! Did Jack peck you again?"

"It couldn't have been him, Mom! He never left us. The bedroom window and the door were shut the whole time," Daniel said, lying like a dog.

"That's true, Aunt Christine. Jack didn't do it!"

"Maybe it was a sparrow… or a parakeet that had escaped from its cage," Bea said, opening her eyes wide.

Tony came to their aid.

"It could have been the neighbor's parrot. Do you remember when it ran away and landed on my windowsill, Mom?"

Christine had no recollection of the incident, no matter how hard she tried. Then again, she was so absent-minded she wasn't surprised.

Gomes was so angry he nearly grinded his teeth. Those pesky, hateful brats! As if anyone could mistake that black crow for a colorful parrot, or a sparrow or a parakeet. He felt like he might take a broom and hit them.

«Well, whaddya know? Naughty boy! Rascal! Hel-lo!», said Jack, looking at Gomes, eyes shining. He burst out laughing, which irritated Gomes even more: he was convinced the crow was smart enough to make fun of him. He imagined all the bad things he would do to it when he had the chance.

"You must find your Father's work very interesting. He's always traveling, getting to know different countries. It must be exciting. Where's he right now? Or is he on vacation somewhere?"

Bea made her most innocent look and broad smile. "Daddy's in the North Pole on a cruise. Mom's gone with him."

Mr. Gomes looked at her, appalled. "The North Pole?! Who would ever want to go on a cruise to the North Pole?!"

"Lots of people—to see the icebergs."

"You're so clumsy, Bea! He went to the South Pole."

Gomes looked at them suspiciously. Could they be speaking the truth? Nope! Nobody would be crazy enough to go on such a cruise. The brats must have been laughing at his expense. The little rascals! The girl, with that angel face, was the worst.

Realizing the others were talking, the cousins also began to make silly comments, preventing Gomes from being able to say anything else. He eventually gave up and raged out the door.

When he was far from prying ears, he dialed a number on his cell phone and waited for someone to answer. A few seconds later, he heard an unpleasant voice.

"I need you to come here, Cruz. So far, I haven't gotten anything out of those kids except a few bites from that wretched crow. I need you to find a way to enter the home of the sister of the owner of the house where I'm staying. She's the boys' godmother. I understand she's very close to our dear Michael Soares. If he got rid of the CD, he must have sent it to his cousin."

«Ok. I'll be there tomorrow. Don't do anything until I tell you. You mustn't attract suspicion».

The next morning was cloudy and muggy. The sun lurked behind the clouds from time to time but shied away again soon after. The four cousins were on their feet before nine o'clock. They had breakfast and ran outside to catch the bus. Each of them bought a nice flashlight. They were excited. They dashed towards the funicular. They had decided to go up to Sítio that morning, to see the famous Chapel of Memory and the great crucifix in the church.

When the funicular started to move, two people hurried up: a woman with a basket full of fruit and cabbages and the mysterious Balthazar Gomes.

"Just my luck! I nearly lost my breath hurrying to catch the funicular and there it goes! Fair winds and fallowing seas to you!" she exclaimed, angry, glaring at the driver. "Why, you little!"

They saw Gomes and looked at each other, annoyed. Jack also spotted him and threw unfriendly adjectives at him. He frowned.

«Rascal! You rascal! Naughty boy! Naughty boy!»

"Is he going to be on our back the whole time?"

"We'll have to lose him every time we want to leave the house. It's no fun having him behind us all the time," Tony said.

The others agreed. They got off the funicular a few moments later. They ran down the wide stairs and headed for the Chapel of Memory. As always, it was packed.

"We should go to the church first. Maybe there'll be less people in the chapel later," Chris suggested, doubtful.

They crossed the square in front of the church, hassled by

vendors trying to sell their wares, went up the semicircular limestone staircase and crossed themselves as they entered the church. They automatically started to speak softly, though they didn't know why. The sun, which had reappeared in the meantime, shone through the multicolored windows. They blinked, marveled at the beauty of it.

"This church has a special ambience, like when we visit a very old monastery," Bea said, admiring everything around her.

"Am… what?" asked Daniel, astonished.

"Atmosphere. What you feel when you come in. It makes you speak softly. It's as if you feel respect for this place," informed Tony.

Daniel understood what he meant.

"It is a very beautiful church!" Chris praised, admiring the tiles on the hallway as they made their way to the sacristy.

The cousins were proud. They stopped at the entrance to the beautiful sacristy. A huge crucifix showing Jesus nailed to it stood out: the statue was big and beautiful. Six pictures depicted the battle between the Moors and the Goths, then the King changing his garments for simple shepherd's clothes. Others depicted the Image hidden between the rocks and the two men, and Dom Rodrigo finding his friend dead on another one.

They were thrilled. They came closer to the altar to look at the base of the great cross. Their eyes widened when they saw what had excited their godmother so much when she was a young girl.

The big black rock showed the cave of the Image of Our Lady of Nazaré in detail. You could see the niche, nicely cut out, where the Image had been found, and caves with underground tunnels and two sets of carved steps at opposite ends, rather than merely those that could be found in the chapel and led all the way down to the niche where the copy of the Image was. The sculpted image of the Friar could be seen there as well. It stood out because its color was similar to the color of candles.

They were breathless and extremely excited. So much emotion had rendered them speechless. All they could do was stare at that fantastic find.

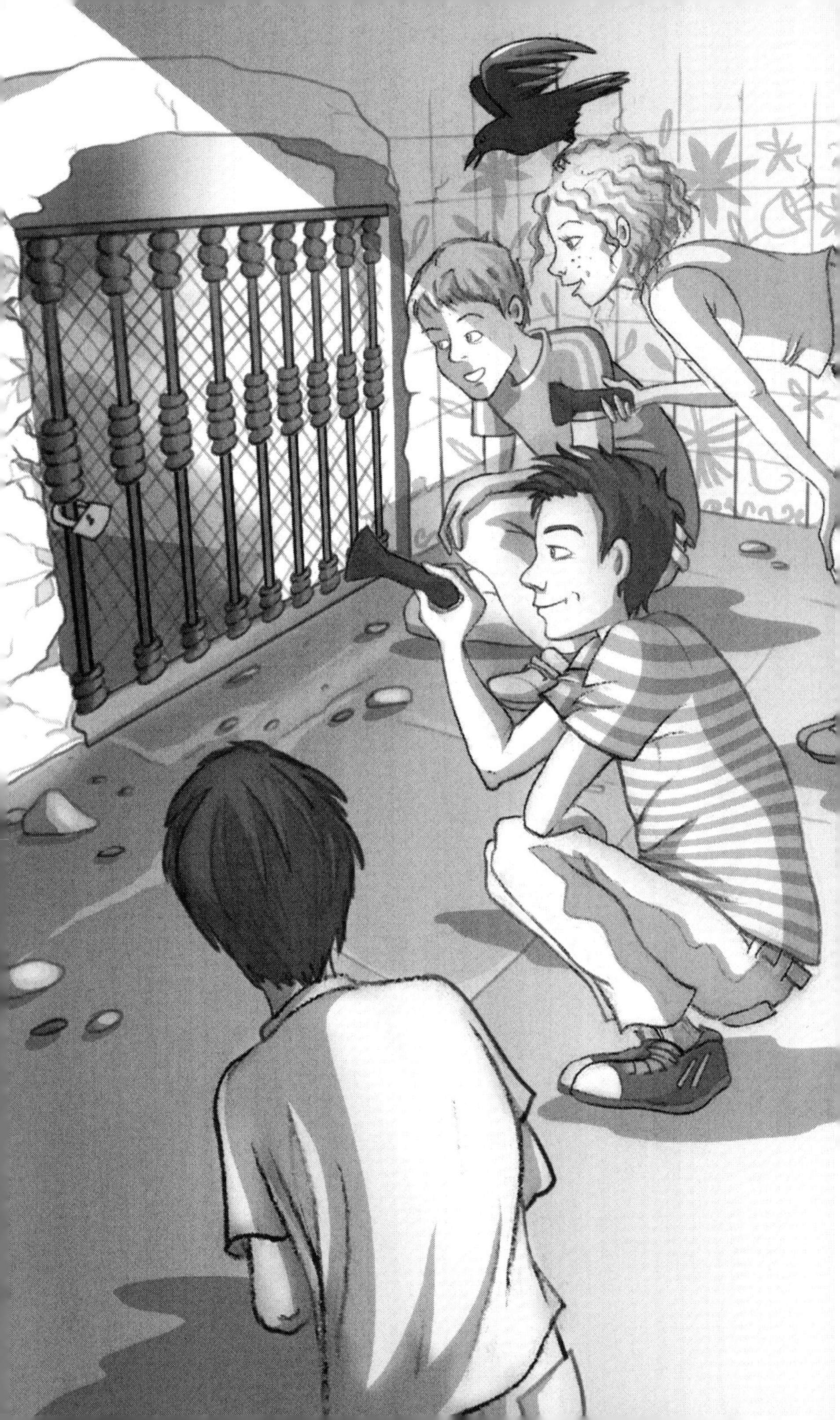

Chapter 10

In the chapel

Tony was the first to break the silence. His keen eye had noticed something that made him exclaim:

"This is not a rock! Look! This bit here is scrapped. It's carved black wood. Maybe it's always been this color, or maybe it got dark over time."

"Perhaps it looked different when Godmom saw it, otherwise she would have realized it was made of wood," Bea commented, her eyes shining.

"Yeah. Have you seen there's a skull on top? What does it mean?" Daniel asked, curious, stretching as much as he could to reach it. "It's cold, so it's not made of wood."

"I wonder if it's Friar Romano's skull."

The others looked at Chris, doubtful.

"Let's go up there and look at the Image!"

A double iron staircase led them to the dressing room where Our Lady of Nazaré stood behind a window case.

They stood before her, watching her closely. She was small, sitting, nursing Baby Jesus. There was a stain on the left side of her face due to the many centuries she had spent in the cave at the mercy of storms and salt air.

"Can you believe how old this Image is? It makes you feel an enormous respect, doesn't it?" Bea said softly, looking keenly at everything.

The boys agreed. They went down the other staircase shortly after. When they were back outside, they went to the Chapel of Memory. Two tourists were on their way out, with cameras on their shoulder, and a woman with a mop and a bucket was cleaning the beautiful old tiles.

As they entered, they saw a crucifix above the altar.

Tony looked at it, puzzled. "This crucifix wasn't here! The last time I was here, there was a big statue where it stands now."

The woman stopped, holding the mop. "It was Our Lady of the Immaculate Conception. It was taken away because it was getting ruined. It's worth a lot, you know?" she informed, then resumed cleaning.

«Hel-lo! Well, whaddya know? Hel-lo!» greeted Jack, who could not stand being silent anymore. He felt he would burst if he carried on that way.

The woman laughed then covered her mouth in embarrassment. She looked around—perhaps she was afraid it was a sin to laugh in that sacred place.

"Shut up, Jack! You can't talk here!" his owner scolded him, patting his beak. He went silent. He didn't like it when that happened. He was a little sulky.

They stood there for a moment, watching everything closely, admiring the tiles and trying to decipher the inscriptions. They gave up eventually: as expected, they were in Latin. They went down the six limestone steps that led to the lower floor carefully, as they couldn't see properly. A small window allowed rays of light to pass through and shine on an Image behind a niche covered by a wire mesh. It was quite colorful, not at all like the one in the Sanctuary.

"This copy of the Image of Our Lady of Nazaré is very different from the one that's in the church. Actually, it couldn't be more different, even though the Virgin is also breastfeeding Baby Jesus!" Bea said, observing it.

The others agreed. They were puzzled, too.

The lady, who was near the stairs, heard the girl and joined them. "This is not Our Lady of Nazaré. They took her to the museum. Everyone thought it was outrageous. This is Our Lady of the Angels," she informed. She looked like she thought the same, too.

"Have you noticed the tiles on the chapel roof depict the famous miracle of Our Lady of Nazaré? There's Dom Fuas Roupinho on horseback chasing the deer, which falls off the cliff..."

Daniel peered out the window, curious. "Did you know you can see the harbor from here? The view is beautiful!"

The others took turns to peek. They almost ran over an old lady who was praying before the Image. They couldn't wait to take a look at the cave below, the entrance to which was covered with bars and locked with a rather rusty chain and padlock. Behind the bars, a wire mesh prevented objects from being thrown into it.

They crouched down to see beyond the opening. Despite all the gloom, they managed to see some candles and other objects scattered on the rock floor.

"Well, whaddya know? How did that get there, with such a tight wire mesh?" Daniel asked, surprised.

"They were probably there before they put the wire mesh."

"Yeah. Godmom didn't mention any wire mesh."

They waited for the old lady to finish her prayer, wishing with all their heart that she would hurry up. When she finally left, Tony and Bea switched on the flashlights. The beam shone inside the cave. They held their breath, thrilled. It was bigger than they had thought, and it seemed to them that the passage to the underground caves might be on the left side. Part of the wall was darker there, which led them to think it might continue there. Their hearts almost jumped out of their chests. Daniel shook the padlock, furious. It was very frustrating not to be able to get inside.

Suddenly, Jack screamed, took off and went out into the open. He had grown tired of all the darkness.

"Well, whaddya know? Now I must go after him. Just my luck!"

Bea left, determined to tell the crow off. She blinked in the sunlight and then looked around. There he was, perched on a basket full of barnacles, chattering to the vendor, who laughed out loud, delighted, and gave him a barnacle. He caught it with his strong beak, flew away with it and landed on the wall over the rocks next to the Chapel of Memory. He began to peck at it, very satisfied, but didn't like the taste of it and threw it out, indignant. It was much too salty! What kind of food was that?

«Rascal! Naughty boy! Scoundrel! Well, whaddya know?»

"You're the scoundrel. Flying away like that!" his owner scolded him. "I think I'll buy some barnacles."

She headed towards the vendor, who was laughing heartily. She was wearing the traditional local clothes and was dark-skinned.

«Hel-lo! Hel-lo! Well, whaddya know? Come, now!» greeted Jack, ending with a little cough, followed by an enormous sneeze. Frightened, a man who was passing by jumped up.

The woman was laughing so hard tears streamed down her face. "Oh, what a priceless bird you have, child! He's the funniest thing I've ever seen! He really is a beauty, he is!"

«He is, he is! Well, whadya know? Come, now!»

The woman laughed even more. She was red now, despite her dark skin tone. She gave the girl a generous portion, hoping she and that funny bird wouldn't go away. She observed him, delighted. It had never crossed her mind that a bird might speak that way.

Jack burst out laughing, mimicking her. She was silent for a moment, only to burst out laughing again. After taking the money from her customer, the vendor ran to the restroom, which was close to the wall between the cliff and the edge.

She asked the vendor from the stall next to hers to mind her stall. She was about to burst, she confided to Bea.

Bea laughed and took a barnacle from the paper cone, peeling it as the vendor had taught her.

"Oh, my God! This is so good! Now, to meet the others. They'll like it, too!"

She ran to meet them. She stopped. The chapel door was closed. "Twenty past twelve", she murmured, looking at her watch. "I wonder if it's closed at lunchtime. I thought it would be open till late in the afternoon. That's weird! Where can they be?"

She went down the steps and looked closely around her. Much to her amazement, they were nowhere to be found. Where were they anyway? Why hadn't they gone to meet her?

«Rascal! You rascal!» Jack said, mimicking Gomes's voice and looking in the direction of the funicular.

Bea followed his gaze. She frowned. She recognized her aunt's lodger, even from behind.

"So that's who you were calling rascal! You saw that idiot. I'm such a fool! Why didn't I suspect it? I wonder if he had the nerve to lock them inside out of revenge for what Daniel did to him. He probably didn't notice it when I left! Rascal! He's been spying on us all along! But why? Does he think we'll just lead him to the CD? Idiot!"

The children had realized they were locked inside the chapel shortly after Bea left in search of the crow. They had grown tired of staring at the entrance to the cave, knowing they didn't stand a chance of getting inside, and decided to go into the sunlight.

"Well, whaddya know? We're locked inside!" Chris said, astonished.

Daniel chuckled, not because he found that bizarre situation amusing, but because he was nervous. He, too, shook the door, thinking that his cousin might not have pushed it strong enough. Then he kicked it.

"I didn't know the chapel was closed at lunchtime!" Tony commented, shining his flashlight on his watch.

"What are we going to do now? We can't stay here, can we?"

"Of course not, Daniel. Don't worry. Bea will be here in no time. She'll help us. We just have to wait a little."

They were silent for a moment, waiting impatiently.

"What if she thinks we left?" Daniel wondered, anxious. He started kicking the door, scaring them.

"Stop it! Don't be such a child, Daniel!"

"Tony! Chris! Daniel! Are you in there?"

The boys looked at each other, relieved.

"Yes, we are, Bea! We're locked inside!"

"Hang on! I'll try to open the door. The bottom bolt's a bit rusty. I did it! I can't get to the top bolt, though. I'm going to ask for help!"

All they heard for a few moments was the chatter of the crow, who had stayed there and was amazed to hear their voices without being able to see them.

Shortly afterwards they heard a noise. Much to their satisfaction, the door opened. They blinked. They had been in that semi-darkness for so long it was hard to get used to daylight. They thanked the man who had opened the door and sat on the wall.

"It was stupid Gomes who locked you up! I saw him leave."

The boys looked at each other, angry.

"It seems to me he's quite dangerous. We must be very careful with him. We don't know what he's capable of," Tony said.

"He must think he's king of the world because he gave us quite a scare. The fool! I feel like pulling the hair off his beard one by one!" said Daniel. His eyes were sparkling with fury.

"We should lose him whenever we can. It's no fun having him right behind us all the time. What a drag!"

"Maybe we should tell Aunt Christine about it."

"He'd deny it, for sure, and say we're lying. Your brother's right, Bea. We must lose him every time we want to go out. I know just how!"

"How?"

"We'll grab our bikes instead of taking the bus. He won't be able to keep up with us, then. He'll be furious!" Tony said, chuckling.

Bea looked at the others, eyes shining. "What if we went straight home and said nothing about what happened? He'd be even more upset, wouldn't he? We'll act as if nothing had happened."

"That's a great idea, Bea! If we can get there first, it'll be even better. He'll be absolutely mad!" Tony said.

"That's it! Let's try to get there first. We'll run a bit from time to time and we'll be there in no time."

"Yeah. That rascal will probably take his time, thinking he got rid of us for a while."

«Rascal! Naughty boy! Scoundrel!»

"That's right, dear. Tell that good-for-nothing scoundrel like it is!" said Chris, with a laugh.

«Good-for-nothing! Scoundrel!» Jack said with a loud laugh.

The children laughed, then went on their way, eating the barnacles. They walked down the road, chatting and laughing until the contents of the paper cone were gone. They ran for a while, stopping when they were tired.

The distance had seemed shorter than it really was. They had always taken the bus, hence the confusion. When they got close to home, they decided to walk at a regular pace, in case Gomes was already there. To Bea and Chris, all the houses in Rio Novo looked the same. They had no idea why their cousins were able to tell theirs. Finally, they spotted the place where they were staying. Sunlight reflected off a lens in the house next door.

"Did you see that? Someone must be watching us. That's weird, isn't it?" Bea asked, suspicious. Who else might be interested in spying on us?"

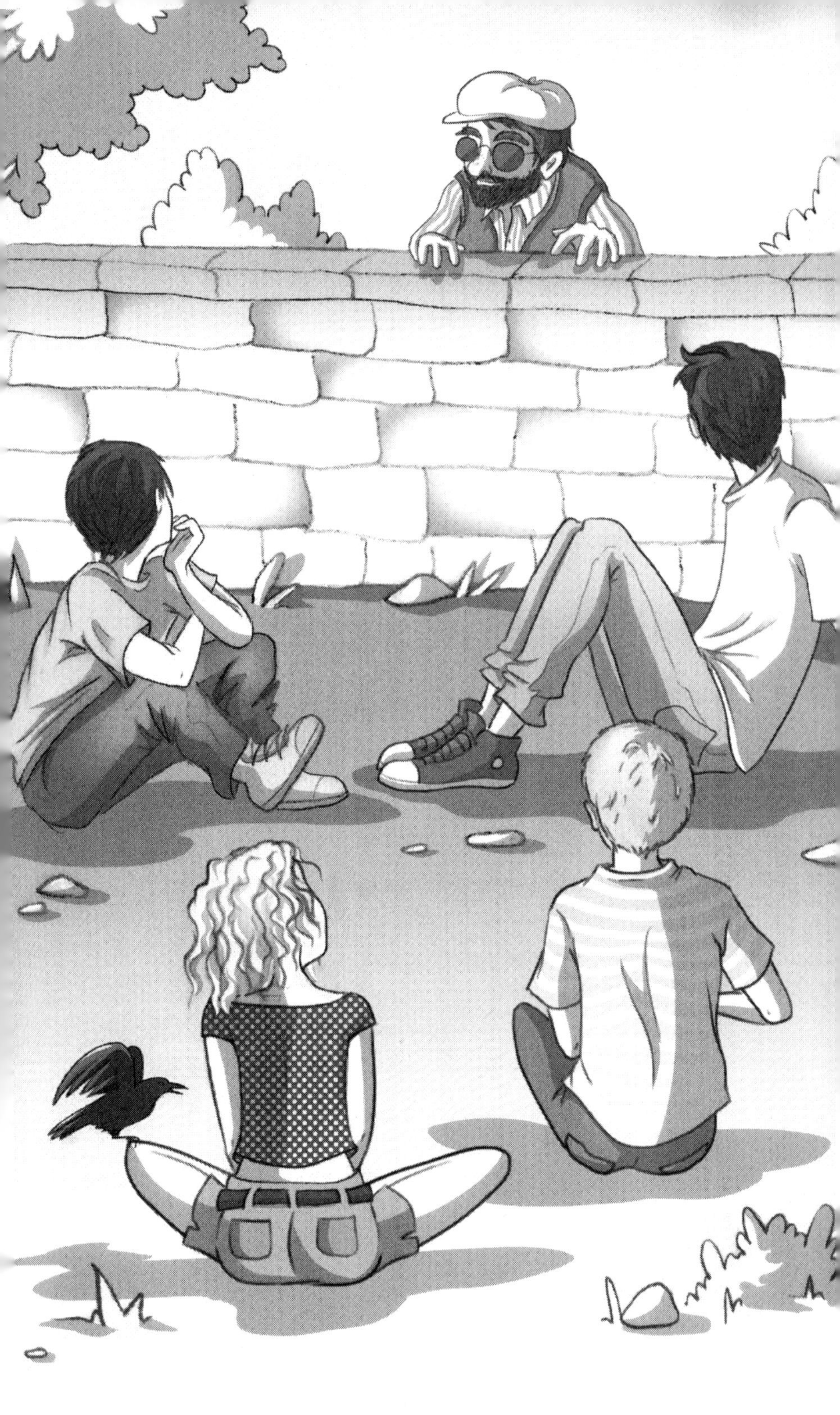

Chapter 11

A different, even more suspicious looking, man

The children shrugged. A few seconds later, the reflection was not there anymore.

"We have to find out who it was!"

They went inside, starving after walking and running so much. They had barely sat down at the table when they realized Gomes had entered. He stopped by the door when he heard their laughter. He gaped. How did they get home first after he locked them inside that chapel?!

"Why don't you join us, Mr. Gomes?"

"No… no, thanks, Mrs. Ricardo. So, back so soon from your little outing?"

«Hel-lo! Naughty boy! Rascal!» Jack said. Gomes was unable to disguise his annoyance when he heard the greeting.

"Did you go for a walk, too, Mr. Gomes?" Bea asked in a sweet tone that made him suspicious. Nosy brats!

"I just stretched my legs. Please excuse me." He went up to his room, determined to take a quick shower so he could follow them later. What a drag! He wouldn't even have time for lunch.

"That guy's a bit weird. I don't like him. I hope he won't stay for long," said the boy's father. He smiled at his nephews.

"So? Do you like it here? It must be very different from what you're used to."

"We like it a lot, Uncle Julian!" said the girl cheerfully. Her brother, who kept himself to himself, nodded.

They helped clear the table after lunch and went to sit on the grass. They talked quietly about the latest events afraid the lodger might overhear them.

Bea, who was the most suspicious of the four, occasionally took a cautious look at the semi-detached villa on the left side of the one they were in. At one point, she seemed to see someone hiding behind a curtain on the first floor, exactly at the same window where she had seen a reflection off the binocular lenses. She motioned to the others and stood up. She walked around the house, moving close to the walls. When she was in the back of the house, she ran towards the road and looked closely at the adjacent house without being seen. Then she went back the same way and joined the others.

"There's a very strange-looking man there spying on us from the window. I don't think he saw me. I wonder what he wants from us."

"Do you think he's Gomes's partner?" Tony asked.

"You could be right. It really is very suspicious, to be spied on by two different men. There has to be a connection," Chris said, taking a sneak peek at the window.

"Did you see what he looked like?"

"No, I didn't. All I saw was he had a beard. Shall we go to the beach this afternoon? The weather is not so overcast anymore."

Chris frowned, but said nothing. He didn't want his sister to call him a killjoy again, and say his cousin was much better company than he was.

Tony noticed his countenance out of the corner of his eye.

"Actually, I thought we should see Forte de São Miguel, the fort where the lighthouse is. The view from there is amazing! Then we could go and see Forno d'Orca. How about it?"

The others agreed. Their eyes were shining.
Suddenly, a strange, ugly-looking face appeared by the wall. They startled. He was forty-something and a little hunched. His belly was tucked in and he wore his pants above the waist, which made him look even weirder. Even though the weather was warm, he wore a wide-striped, long-sleeve shirt and a sleeveless cardigan. His short pants showed his ankles and his feet. Strangely enough, he was wearing socks and sandals. His hands were large and very pale. His face looked even stranger: he had a bushy black beard (not very well-groomed—you couldn't see his lips); a thick nose, red and full of black spots, and bushy eyebrows; his eyes were hiding behind round-rimmed, dark-lensed glasses. He was wearing a cap that could do with a wash over rather greasy brown hair.

"Hello, children! My name is Abel Cruz."

They stared at him. They weren't happy. They didn't like it when someone called them children. Besides, he had a rather unpleasant voice. They wondered if he had been there for a long time and whether he had overheard their conversation.

"Are you all brothers and sisters?" he asked, with a smile that showed his teeth, which were a little protruding, like a rabbit's.

"Yes, we are," Bea replied dryly. She turned and looked at the others, intent on ignoring him. He seemed to think otherwise.

"That's funny. You don't look like you are."

"Each of us has a different mother," Chris replied, serious.

The man gaped, astonished. He resumed his questioning after a brief silence. "Is the beach alright?"

"Yeah, it is."

"You see, I have chronic bronchitis and I need to sunbathe. It seems sunbathing's good for my condition. I'd never been to Nazaré before. I've been told the beach is beautiful, though I think it probably is no match for the beaches in the Algarve. The water is pleasantly warm there, which I don't think is the case here."

"Then maybe you should go there," Tony said in an unpleasant tone.

The man giggled, which annoyed them even more. "I was there last year, kid. I decided to head this way this year."

"What a pity," Daniel commented, rudely.

The man cocked his head. "What was it you said, kid? I'm a little deaf in this ear. I also have rheumatism. You'll know what it's like when you're as old as I am! What's that bird called? It's a blackbird, isn't it?"

"Of course not! It's a crow! Blackbirds are much smaller," Bea replied dryly, appalled at his ignorance. Her nose twitched when she saw his oily hair.

"Oh! They like to hide things, don't they?"

Much to the children's relief, another man came from the same house and joined him.

"There's a call for you," he announced.

He looked much nicer than the other man. He was of medium height, with a big belly, and his clothes were simple, but tasteful. He was about 50. His mouth was big, with big teeth, and he had gray, rough hair. He had a captivating smile. As soon as he saw the man hurrying back to the house, he turned to them, smiling.

"Hi, guys! My name's Jack Pereira. I hope you haven't been sharing secrets. Mr. Cruz had been crouching behind the wall for some time.

They looked at each other, annoyed and angry.

"The nerve of him!"

"You're right! I'd be as furious as you are. Don't tell him too much. He likes snooping around. He wants to know everything!"

"We know what you mean," Tony said, giving him a friendly look.

"Make sure he's not around when you wish to talk."

"Thanks for the warning, Mr. Pereira."

"Please call me Jack. I like it better. Call me anytime!"
They also introduced themselves. He seemed nice.
«Hel-lo! Well, whaddya know?» Jack said his usual greeting.
Mr. Pereira laughed out loud. Jack did the same.
"What a nice crow you have there!"
The strange-looking man came back, puzzled. "There was no call for me."
"You don't say! Maybe the call went down. Well, see you later, guys! Don't forget what I told you!"
The four cousins tried not to laugh. They had understood their new friend had played a prank on the nosy man.
They realized Gomes was behind them.
"Have you seen my glasses? I left them on my bed when I went to shower. They weren't there when I came back."
«Naughty boy! Rascal! Scoundrel!» Jack shouted close to his ears.
Gomes frowned angrily. He wanted to twist his neck so much!
"We haven't seen them, Mr. Gomes."
He looked suspiciously at the crow.
"What about that... bird? It might have taken them."
"I don't think Jack likes to wear sunglasses," Bea said in a very sweet tone.
Gomes frowned, angry. He went back inside. He could her them laugh. Even the other man smiled.
They hopped on their bikes a bit later. They were carrying a snack in their backpacks. They had told their mother they were off to Sítio: they said nothing about Forno d'Orca so as not to worry her. Mothers are always ready to worry about something.
The lodger, who was watching them from the window, went outside to follow them. A hoarse voice called him from over the wall.
"It's Mr. Gomes, isn't it? Those children were very rude to you a while ago. They were indeed! They get no education from their parents, that's what it is! Back in the old days, children would never dare speak to an adult like that. Don't you agree?"

Gomes nodded. He was intent on pursuing the young adventurers. He felt like covering that boring man's mouth. He just didn't know how.

"Are you here for health reasons, Mr. Gomes? I am, unfortunately. I'm a very sick person, you know? I have chronic bronchitis, rheumatism..."

Gomes was not interested in his ailments at all. He just wanted to follow the children. It was too late for that now. They were making good progress. All because of that motor mouth!

He went back inside, muttering something. He didn't even notice the other man was smiling. Meanwhile, the four children were pedaling furiously. They slowed down a bit after a while, as they saw no one was behind them.

"That Mr. Cruz surely looks terrible!"

"He looks disgusting, too. Can you picture him having soup with that beard? It must get dirty all over. I don't think he'll take the trouble to wash it," Bea said, looking disgusted.

"Do you think he overheard our conversation?" Chris asked.

"I don't think so. He said he was deaf in one ear. Perhaps that was his intention, but we were chatting softly," his cousin replied. "The rascal!"

"I was surprised Jack didn't pluck some hair off his beard, as he did the other one," Daniel said, laughing.

They laughed as well.

"That's funny. I was waiting for that to happen all the time, too," Tony said, looking interestedly at the crow that was flying beside his owner. "The truth is he behaved very well. He was as quiet as a mouse, looking at the man with his head cocked, as if he were very interested in what he was saying."

Bea was thoughtful. "It really is strange. I hope he's not getting sick or something."

Her brother laughed. "Don't be a fool! How could poor Jack say anything! That guy just kept talking! Jack must have been completely stunned."

«Fool! Naughty boy! Well, whaddya know?»

They laughed heartily. From then on, the crow didn't shut up along the way, screaming, laughing, sneezing and coughing. He seemed to be completely crazy.

They got to Sítio a few minutes later. They went down the road that led to the fort, feeling the wind in their faces. Even in hot weather, it was nearly always windy there—even more so in winter.

They stopped before the fort, leaned their bikes against the wall and locked them together. Anyone who dared to steal one of the bikes would have to take them all, which would be extremely difficult and tiring.

There were several cars parked there and many tourists, Portuguese as well as foreigners.

Tony took a rough path to the left and went down cautiously. The others followed him. It led to a wall with shells embedded on the cement, as if it were a balcony over the sea. The view was simply wonderful! In the distance, you could see the harbor, the seaside road, the buildings, and the beach packed with tourists and people bathing in the sea. A fresh breeze ruffled their hair and Jack's feathers. He wasn't happy.

"Look! Have you seen the shape of that huge rock sticking out of the cliff? It looks so strange!" Bea pointed excitedly. "It looks like a—"

"—a frog!" Tony added, laughing. We think so, too."

They stood there for a few moments admiring the strange shape. Then they went up, trying not to lose their footing. They headed towards the other end, enjoying the beautiful landscape overlooking Praia do Norte.

"Look! There's Forno d'Orca!" Daniel pointed, excited. Everyone felt the same. Their eyes shone brightly in anticipation of the pleasure they would fell when they explored that unique-shaped cave. They couldn't wait for it.

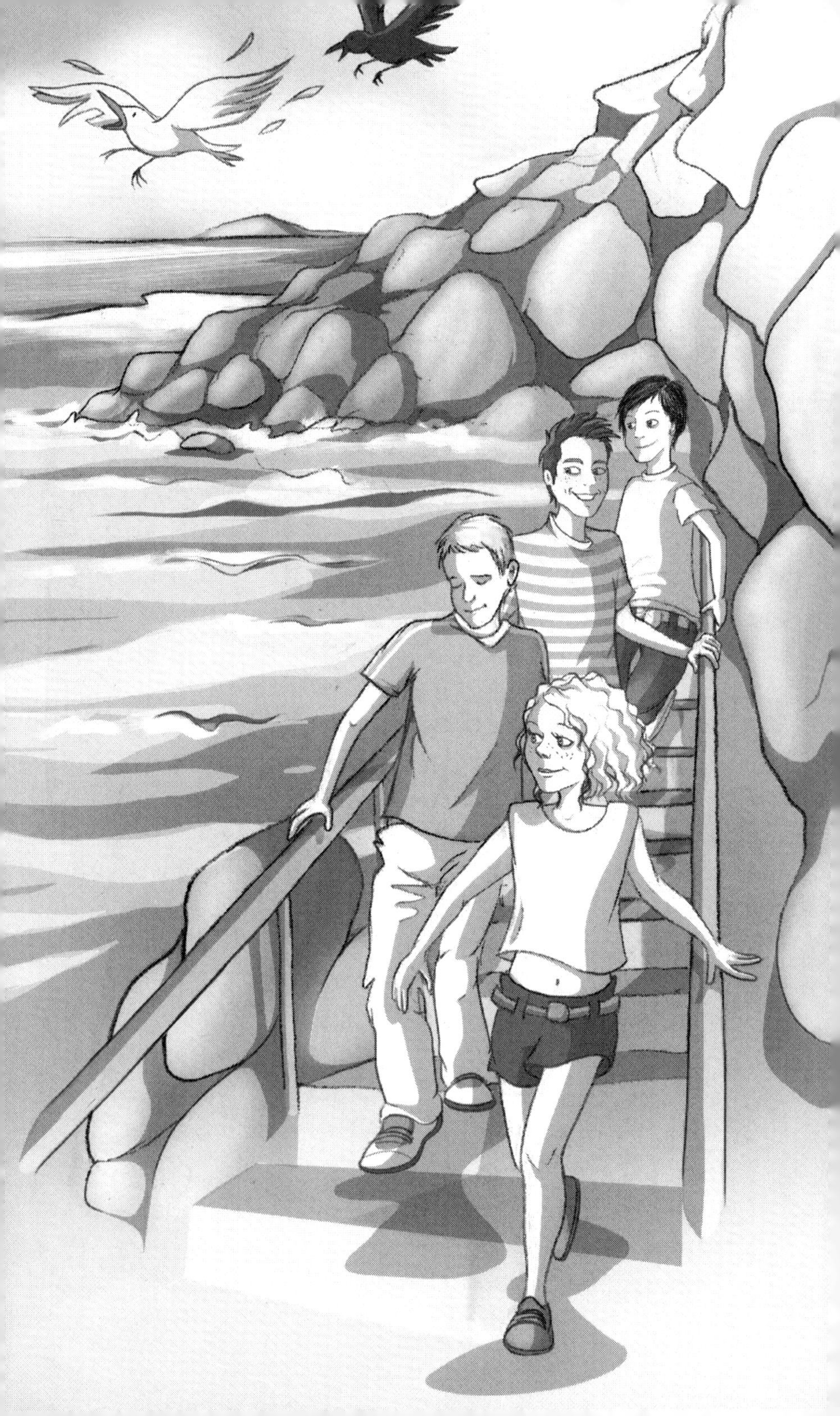

Chapter 12

At Forte de São Miguel and Forno d'Orca

The children went down the stairs carved in the rock. They led to an iron staircase painted blue, suspended in the air and quite steep, which made Chris dizzy. He decided he wouldn't mention it to his cousins, afraid they might call him chicken.

They made their way down carefully, clinging to the handrails. They would stop for a few seconds, then take another flight of steps.

They were now standing on the rock. They treaded carefully: as you'd imagine, the sea had made the rocks slippery and very uneven.

They approached the wall that was used as a belvedere over the sea and observed the huge rock that stood before them, which the locals called Pedra do Guilhim. Opposing currents gathered in a whirlwind between it and the rock where the fort had been built. The noise was ceaseless, and the spectacle majestic. The huge sea spread out as far as the eye could see.

They leaned over carefully. The cave their great-grandmother had told them about should be directly below them, deep down. Perhaps it was the meeting place for pirates from the days of yore when the sea receded many years ago.

For a moment they let themselves be carried away by their imagination. How exciting it must have been to live back then! The spray from the waves breaking at the base of the fort wetted their faces and hair. They didn't care—they even liked it. They looked at each other, smiling, realizing that they were all thinking the same.

They climbed the rock they had come down only moments ago and passed through an arch carved on the rock. Luckily, their sneakers had rubber soles, otherwise they would certainly slip. Curiously, the sound of the waves seemed to come from deep inside the rock where the fort stood. They had a strange feeling.

"It seems you can hear the waves better on this rock, doesn't it?" Bea asked, looking at the others.

They agreed and resumed their way carefully. Further up there was another belvedere overlooking the sea. They were delighted with the view. It was so beautiful it took their breath away! The sea, the beach, Pederneira, Monte de São Brás, the cliff and the toad-shaped rock, Pedra do Guilhim...

Three fishermen were standing there, holding their fishing rods, and looking serious. They were not pleased with the arrival of four children and a bird that was even noisier than the gulls. The gulls looked at the crow, amazed. Jack mimicked their screams perfectly, which disoriented them. Surely, they must be relatives: they all spoke the same language. He was probably a distant cousin.

When Jack started meowing like a cat, they flew away screaming, scared. They were even more haunted when they heard him laugh out loud, like those humans who walk on two legs do. The children almost burst out laughing. Even the fishermen smiled, although they wished with all their heart that they wouldn't stay there too long. They'd scare the fish away—of that they were sure.

They carefully retraced their steps. After some time, they found themselves standing before the fort. They were panting.

They sat on the wall for a while to gain back their strength, as there was still a lot of walking to be done. It was a long way down to Forno d'Orca.

"Come on, you lazy guys!" Tony said, jumping to the ground and standing up.

«Lazy guys! Well, whaddya know?»

"That's right, Jack. Show them!"

They set out. They noticed they were treading on clay-colored ground. There was undergrowth and a few flowers scattered here and there.

As they went down, the cliff behind them seemed to be getting higher. Some tourists were also heading to Praia do Norte, with a towel on their shoulders and a shoulder bag. The children had some trouble walking down the narrow paths. Then they reached some narrow steps. They ended up at the top of the so-called Forno d'Orca. It was a relatively large, round-shaped cave with no roof. There were protrusions in the upper part, big enough for an adult to lie inside.

They leaned over, looking down, and exclaimed excitedly. Jack flew over the large opening, screaming like a gull, outraged. The children seemed to have forgotten about him. It was unfair. Were those rocks really worth paying no attention to him?!

They went down a kind of rough steps made of cement. Sometime later they were inside Forno d'Orca. They took off their sneakers because of the sand and walked around, excited, exploring all the openings and talking to each other.

"There's water dripping all the time. Have you noticed?" Bea said, running her hands over the rock. She touched a finger to her tongue, curious. "It's not salty. I wonder if you can drink it."

"We don't know. Don't do it again," her brother scolded her. "It could be sewage water."

"Don't be stupid! In that case, it would certainly taste and smell bad."

"It may not be good to drink. Just leave it."

"The sea gets here in the winter. The same thing happens down there on the beach. One minute, tourists are walking on the wall, then, suddenly, they're surprised by the waves. It's so funny to watch them running, trying to hold on to their shoes and their cameras," Tony said, laughing.

The cousins laughed, picturing the scene.

"Now, there's a sight worth seeing! Sometimes the waves hit the streets, too. It's so cool!" Daniel said, bursting out laughing as he recalled it.

Bea and Chris laughed even more. They promised themselves they'd return to Nazaré in the winter to watch that unique spectacle. It must be so exciting!

"Sometimes the waves are so high they climb over Pedra do Guilhim and crash against the lighthouse."

"Wow! That must be great!" Bea exclaimed, her green eyes shining with excitement. Her brother agreed, imagining it.

"Do you think we can try to find the cave Zazabeth told us about?"

Tony shook his head. "The tide is high. We can only go there when there's no water inside the cave. I'll ask Dad when the tide's low tomorrow."

"We can take a look at the openings in the rocks, though. Aren't you coming, Bea?" her brother asked when he saw she wasn't following them.

"I'll be right there. I want to take another look up there. Do you want to come, Daniel?"

He agreed. They went away, chatting, while the others went to the beach, silent.

The younger children explored the area above, stepping into the openings, amused. Suddenly, Daniel looked towards the road to Sítio and stopped, suspicious. He spotted someone holding something in his hands. He was sure what it was when he saw the sunlight reflecting off a lens.

"Look over there, Bea!"

"Rats! It's Mr. Cruz, spying on us. Rascal! How did he get up here so quickly?! He must have driven there."

«Rascal! Naughty boy! Well, whaddya know?» said Jack, looking like he understood what they were saying.

Suddenly, he took flight from his owner's shoulder and dashed towards the man, shouting something they didn't understand.

"What's wrong with him?"

"I hope he pecks his nose!" Daniel said with a wry smile.

"He can harm him, if we're not around."

Their mouths gaped when they saw the crow flutter around the man, screaming. It didn't look like he was going to peck him. The man didn't seem angry at all. He seemed to be amused. He ended up turning his back and walking away up the road slowly, realizing the children had spotted him. Jack flew beside him for a moment before he flew back to his owner.

"Traitor! Making friends with the enemy! Shame on you!" his owner told him off. "Get away from me!"

«Shame on you! Shame on you! Wake up, you lazy girl! Wake up, you lazy girl!»

Daniel laughed. He was beginning to think the crow was really funny. To his delight, Jack landed on his shoulder. He was ecstatic.

"No one was sleeping, you crazy bird!"

«Crazy bird! Naughty boy! Rascal! Shame on you!»

They went to join the others, laughing, trying not to get sand on the people lying on their towels to get a tan. They told them what had happened. They were all worried.

"That rascal's going to follow us no matter where we go," Chris said, frowning. "Are you sure it was Cruz?"

"Of course I am. You can't mistake him for anyone else," Bea said dryly.

"We must face it. Gomes or Cruz will follow us wherever we go. We managed to get rid of one of them this time, but the other one overheard our conversation. We must be careful from now on," Tony decided, looking serious.

"You guys wanna grab a bite? Walking has whetted my appetite!" Daniel confessed, looking at them anxiously.

"Good idea! I'm hungry, too!"

"I could eat a horse!"

Bea laughed. Her cousin was right. She was starving as well.

They unzipped their backpacks and took out cheese sandwiches, packs of juice—which were no longer cold—and a little box of cherries for each one. Jack was delighted when he saw the cherries. He loved them. He feasted on them for some time. His owner's t-shirt was now full of cherry stains.

"How can you eat so much, Tony? Is there a hole in our stomach or something?" Chris asked, looking at him in awe.

Tony laughed. "I'm just growing up, that's all. I need to eat a lot!"

"Your house will be too small for you, if you keep on growing up like that!" Bea commented with a good-natured laugh. She had learned to like her big, grub-munching cousin. He was really cool. "Move over, Jack! I'm all sticky! You're such a sloppy mess!"

«Sloppy! Sloppy! Mess!» the crow shouted, delighted by the sound of that new word. People nearby laughed.

Much to his indignation, he had dropped the cherry on the sand when he opened his beak. He grabbed it again, but immediately threw it away. He hated the taste of sand.

Chris looked at his sister. He was astonished. He had never heard her say that word before—only their aunt. He wondered if Bea was slowly losing her manners, too. She was already beginning to talk like them.

His sister realized by his look what he was thinking. She laughed. "Don't be so serious, Chris. You must agree this word is great! Sloppy. Sloppy! I feel like saying it lots of times! It's a shame I can't say it just because!"

Their cousins laughed. Even her brother ended up smiling.

A few minutes later, they decided to return and started to climb in a single line. They got on their bikes and cycled towards the square in front of the church.

When they got to the belvedere, they leaned over it, looking at the precipice. The most prominent part of the cliff was Bico da Memória, the so-called Edge of Memory where the chapel was built and where, according to legend, Dom Fuas Roupinho's miracle had taken place.

"Do you want to see the mark left by Dom Fuas Roupinho's horse on the rock?" Daniel asked excitedly.

His cousins looked at him, doubtful.

"I'm not kidding. There's a round mark there. Old people say it was left by his horse when it was about to fall off the cliff," Tony said, smiling. "Come on! I'll show you where it is!"

They left their bicycles nearby and climbed up. It was a bit hard to get there. The rock was uneven. They leaned over the left side of the wall and then they saw the famous mark the locals swear is proof that there was indeed a miracle. Bea was thrilled with the discovery. Her brother twitched his nose. He just couldn't bring himself to believe it.

They got home sometime later. To their amazement, Abel Cruz was leaning over the wall, talking to their mother. He smiled broadly when he saw them. "So, did you have a nice time?"

"Yeah," said Chris, dryly. "What about you? Did you have a nice time, too?"

"I just stayed here. My rheumatism is killing me. What can I say?"

The children looked at him, indignant. They knew all too well they had seen him on the road, watching them through his binoculars. Liar! He could probably walk just as well as they did.

"Mr. Cruz found our lodger's glasses," Christine said, pleased, showing them the glasses. They were so full of dust they were almost beyond recognition. She cleaned them with a handkerchief for a while.

"Your bird must have hidden them! Those birds love hiding things," he said, looking like an expert.

"Did you see it with your binoculars, Mr. Cruz?"

"Oh! No, but—" he started to say, but realizing he had been caught, he cleared his throat, serious, and looked at them suspiciously.

"You like to spy on other people through your binoculars, don't you, Mr. Cruz?"

"Where did you get that crazy idea, kid? Of course not! I don't like snooping around."

"I beg to differ," Daniel muttered.

Cruz looked at him, suspicious, which meant he realized what he had said. He wasn't as deaf as he claimed to be after all.

They went inside, just as Gomes was coming down the stairs.

"Your next-door friend here found your glasses."

He grabbed his glasses and stared at Tony, puzzled.

"Friend?! What friend?! I don't know anyone next door!"

"You seemed to be chatting as if you were good friends a while ago," Chris said.

"Oh, that guy! I'd never seen him before! He's so boring!"

With those words, Gomes went back upstairs, suspecting the crow had been behind the disappearance of the glasses. He headed for the bathroom, where he spent a good ten minutes getting rid of all the dirt on his glasses.

Jack saw the open window and flew towards it. He landed on the windowsill. He looked curiously at the strange object and tried to grab it with his strong beak, to no avail. He finally succeeded at the very moment Gomes was entering the bathroom. Gomes stood there staring at him, for a moment, speechless. Finally, he let out a scream that scared Jack. The bird took off, trying hard to hold the cell phone.

"Fiend! Damn bird!"

When he opened his beak to repeat what he had heard, Jack dropped the cell phone on the grass, much to Gomes's anger and dismay. He ran down the stairs so quickly he almost collided, head-first, with the door.

Gomes grabbed his cell phone and punched in a few numbers. It had broken down for good. He was furious. He threatened the bird with a clenched fist.

"You rascal! I'll show you what's good for you! You just wait!" he muttered.

He saw something moving out of the corner of his eye and turned. The eccentric lodger next door was watching him with a wry smile on his face, which irritated him even more.

Someone else had also seen what had happened and cringed, laughing. It was Daniel, who ran to tell the others. They laughed their heads off. When he was on his way back to his room, Gomes suspected he knew why they were laughing so much.

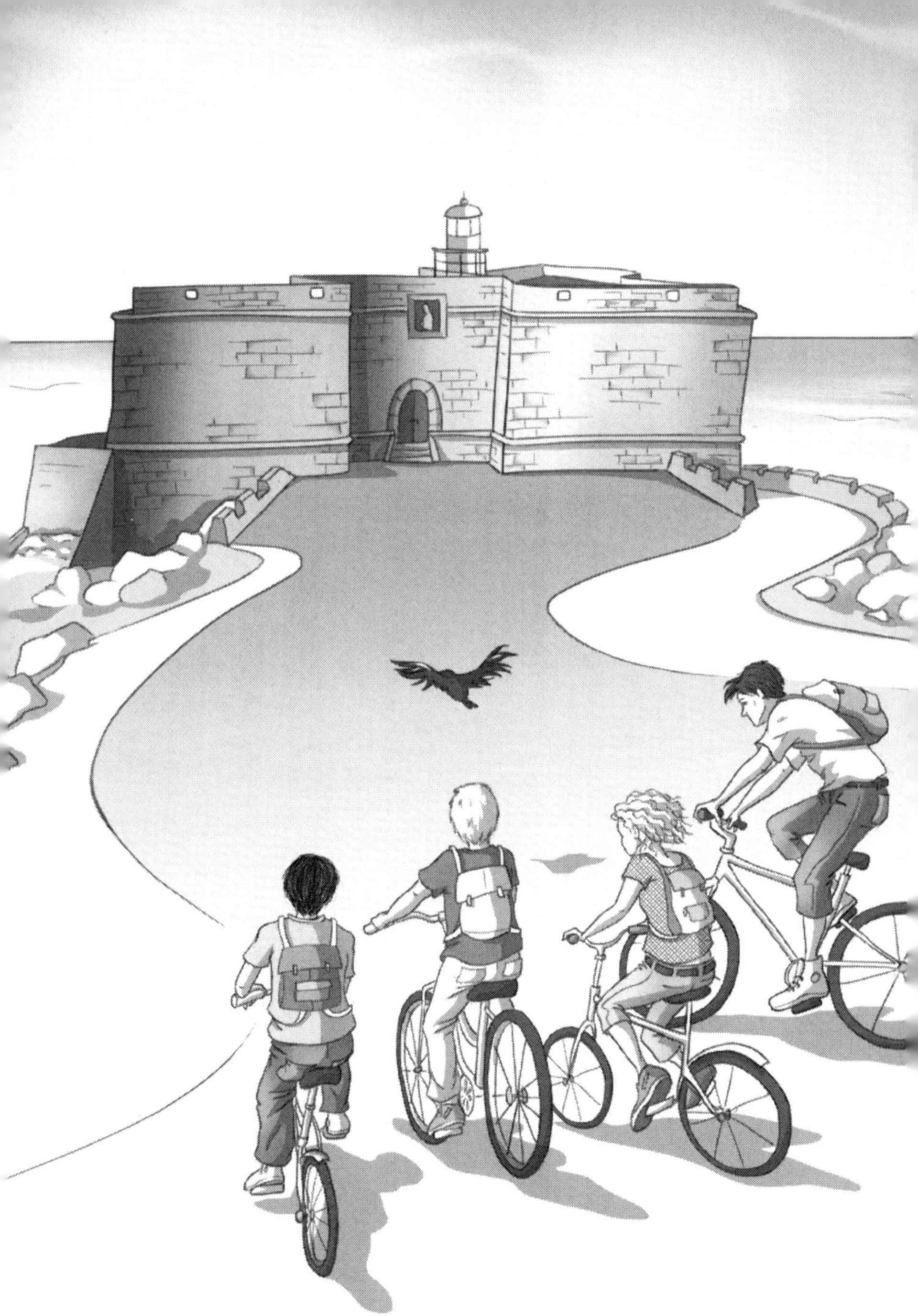

Chapter 13

The Cave!

The heat was stifling that night. Bea tossed and turned in her bed. She couldn't bring herself to sleep. She got up to have some water and cool her face, then went back to bed. Finally, she went to the window, waiting for sleep to come.

It was a beautiful night, even though there was no full moon. Suddenly, she heard a whisper. It seemed to come from the porch. She stuck her head out and tried to look. Two people were standing next to the wall between the semi-detached houses, one on each side of the wall. They were chatting softly. They looked around cautiously from time to time.

She stepped back. Her heart was pounding inside her chest. She headed towards her cousins' room and shook the older one. He looked at her, confused.

"What is it, Bea?"

"Gomes and the next-door lodger are whispering outside. The liar! He said he didn't know him. They seem to be conspiring."

"Did you hear what they were saying?"

She shook her head, discouraged. Tony got up and peered, too. He could barely make out two people leaning against the wall.

"Go to bed. We'll talk about it tomorrow."

"Let's lock him outside again," she said, smiling.

His cousin laughed.

"Better not. We mustn't make him feel agitated."

The next morning, they talked quietly about the previous night's events. Daniel and Chris were a little sulky because they didn't wake them up. No for long, though: after all, they would try to find the cave that morning.

"Do you know what time the low tide is?" Bea whispered in her cousin's ear.

"At eleven o'clock."

At about ten o'clock, after breakfast was over, the phone rang. Tony answered. He then motioned for the others to come closer.

"It's Zaza. She wants to know what our lodger looks like," he informed, listening carefully to what she was saying. "No, he isn't. He's thin and he has a beard."

He hung up after a few more words. He called the others and motioned them to a corner of the room.

"What happened?" they asked, excited.

"A man went to visit Zaza yesterday. He said he worked in the forestry services and he'd like to see how the construction work on the house went. She suspected it was Gomes, so she asked me what he looked like. He was someone else entirely. Zaza was relieved. She also told me he stayed for some time. He took a souvenir from Agnes when he left, though," he told them, laughing.

"What do you mean?"

"While they were talking at the kitchen table, Agnes had fun painting his shoes with Andy's gouaches. Zaza said they were a true work of art."

They laughed, amused. They told their aunt the little girl's latest prank.

She laughed, too.

They left a few moments later and rode their bicycles with their backpacks. Much to their relief, they weren't followed.

The weather was overcast and muggy. They made most of the way in silence, pleased. They got to Sítio sometime later.

They cycled full steam ahead down the road. Then they saw the beautiful fort and the encircling sea. There were no cars there.

They carefully parked their bikes, locked them together and almost flew down the path to the beach.

They stopped for a few moments to wonder at Forno d'Orca once more and then jumped onto the sand. They looked around. A few people were scattered on the immense beach, shivering a little whenever the sun had the nerve to let itself be obscured by clouds.

They laid down their backpacks and covered them with their towels. They were all wearing shorts and t-shirts. Then they turned and looked at the rocks. Their eyes were shining. They hoped from the bottom of their hearts they'd find the cave their Godmother had told them about.

They ran barefoot towards the rocks and began to explore all the openings they could find. There were a lot of them. They had a lot of fun. Besides, the crow seemed to be even crazier than usual. He'd burst out laughing, then cough, then mimic Gomes telling them off. He seemed as excited as they were, as if he had been infected by their enthusiasm.

"Look at this opening!" Daniel called, getting inside.

He reappeared a few minutes later, panting. He looked at the others, smiling.

"It's a bit tight in there. I thought I'd get stuck."

They laughed and headed for the waterline, climbing carefully onto the rocks.

Chris had a little trouble keeping the balance. He wasn't as used to so much physical exercise as his cousins were. Unlike his sister, he didn't like it that much.

"Come have a look! Quick! I think I found it!" Bea shouted excitedly, waiting for the sea to recede for a few seconds and entering through a hole.

The boys looked around. They couldn't see her, but they could hear her muffled voice. Only after some time did they realize where she was. They saw her coming out through the rocks, getting wet up to her knees.

"Is that it?"

"I think so! Come have a look!"

"Is it safe? The sea goes all the way there," Chris said, anxious.

"Don't be afraid, Chris. The tide's still going down. We won't get trapped there. Come on!" Tony said, smiling. Is there room for all of us in there, Bea?"

"It's not too wide. I'll get out. Then you can come in, one at a time."

As soon as she came out, Tony went in, bending down slightly so as not to hit his head on the rock. For a moment, he couldn't see anything. Only after he got accustomed to the darkness inside, was he able to see something.

"Here! Here's a flashlight," Daniel said, poking his head into the opening, panting. "I took it from my backpack."

"Good idea, Daniel. It's very dark in here," the boy said, pointing the beam of light around him. A pile of rocks stood opposite. It was high enough for someone to walk on it. They continued right into the cliff, curving to the left. He pointed his flashlight to the ground. There was a deep round hole to his right. Light sand was shining.

"Can we get in now, Tony? I'm dying to have a look!" Daniel exclaimed anxiously.

His brother laughed and went out. His eyes shone with excitement. "You were right, Bea! This is it! I'll be damned if there's no way out! Be careful! There's a deep hole in the ground!"

Daniel almost snatched the flashlight from his hands and went inside, watching everything closely. Then it was Chris's turn and, finally, Bea's. Jack didn't like the experience at all but remained on the shoulder of his beloved owner. He didn't want to be left out.

"Can we explore it now, Tony? Can we?" Bea asked, looking excitedly at her cousin as soon as they all met outside. The waves were hitting their feet.

"Maybe we should get ready for it first. We should bring ropes and some food. We may have to be inside for a while and do some walking as well."

"We can ask Mom to get us food. We'll tell her we're going to spend the whole day at the beach," Daniel said.

"That's a good idea. Don't look at me that way, Bea! Be wise! Can't you see we don't know what we'll find? We have to be ready for any eventuality," Chris said. When he saw his younger cousin's puzzled gaze, he added: "Anything that may happen."

Tony looked at his watch. He almost jumped.

"Rats! It's been over an hour! Mom will be mad at us! Come on, get your things and run!"

And so they did. They were almost breathless by the time they reached the road. They raced towards their bikes. Fortunately, they were still there. They hopped on, exhausted. They were so worried they didn't say a word all the way. They feared Christine's reaction, seeing them get home so late. She must be worried sick, and they had reasons for it.

They got home a few minutes before two. They went into the kitchen, gazing at their shoes.

Christine, hands on her hips, gave them a disapproving look. "Aren't you a bit late for lunch? I thought you'd be drowned by now! Now, you'll have lunch just the way it is—I don't care if it's cold or warm. Oh, and, by the way, you're grounded for the rest of the day! No beach for you tomorrow either! You're lucky it's Tony's birthday tomorrow."

They looked down and didn't reply. They knew all too well she was right. They were angry at themselves for forgetting the time. Now they would have to wait for two days to explore the cave. That would be their true punishment!

They apologized, gazing at their shoes, and ate in silence. «Naughty boys! Rascals! Shame on you! Well, whaddya know?» Jack said, mimicking Christine and ending with a discreet cough.

She laughed and patted the funny bird's head. She gave him a dish packed with cherries. He was delighted. She looked at the children out of the corner of her eye. They looked so sad and sorry she felt sorry for them. She was calmer now she wasn't worried anymore. In addition to her children, she was in charge with two other children. As much as she wanted to undo what she had said, she refrained from doing it. It would be better that way. They would have to learn to be more responsible from now on. Still, it broke her heart to see them looking like that. She could still recall how it was when she was young: time went by so quickly when she was having fun.

Once the meal was over, they got together in one of the bedrooms, gloomy. They didn't even feel like talking. Jack did all the talking. He was delighted that no one told him to shut up. He had a great time mimicking all the words and noises he knew. The children ended up feeling a little less sad, what with all the nonsense he said.

"I didn't know it was your birthday tomorrow," Bea said, looking at her cousin.

"To be honest, I was so excited I'd forgotten all about it. Cheer up! Let's get everything we need for our expedition ready. You'll see how time flies!"

It didn't. They were all too disappointed and cranky. A violent argument broke out between Bea and Daniel.

"I can't believe how stuck-up you are! You'd think you guys

keep everything tidy and are no trouble at all! And you're so touchy-feely! You keep criticizing the way we speak! You two should be ashamed for being so stuck-up!" Daniel exclaimed, glaring at his cousin.

"You should be ashamed of your room! What a dump!" Bea said. Her eyes were flashing. "You think your mother is your slave! I feel sorry for her! You never ever help her! No wonder she sometimes looks so tired."

Daniel pursed his lips, furious.

"Our lives are none of your business! This is not your house. We're not used to making our beds and dusting, like you are!"

"Well, you should be! Aunt Christine wouldn't have to work like a slave for you all the time then! You surely have a funny way of showing her you love her!"

Her cousins were speechless. No one had ever said that to them. They had never realized how selfish they were. They bit their lips as they realized how tired their mother usually looked. Taking care of four children, a husband and a lodger and cleaning all the house was no picnic.

"Shut up, Bea! You're not home. You can't speak like that. You have such a short fuse! Daniel has a point: we're also giving Aunt Christine a lot of work, even though we tidy up our room. You know well Jack can be a mess sometimes," her brother scolded her, annoyed.

Bea bit her lip to keep from crying.

"I always try to clean up after Jack. I don't wait for Aunt Christine to do it. If that ever happened, it was because I didn't see it! You should have called my attention right away, instead of rubbing it in my face now!"

Tony and Chris looked at each other. They felt uncomfortable. They didn't know what to say to calm them down. They were both in a bad mood and sulking, eager to get to each other's throat. The two older children felt truths had been said on both sides, which was why they were embarrassed.

Christine, who had rushed upstairs when she heard angry voices, had stopped to listen to their argument. She ended up tiptoeing back downstairs. Let them settle their differences, she thought.

They went to bed early, still sulking. When they woke up the next morning, the previous day's argument seemed very silly to them. They had breakfast, still embarrassed, but after apologizing to one another, everything was at peace.

Christine smiled. She was satisfied. The argument had not been a complete waste of time after all. She had been pleasantly surprised when she entered her sons' room that morning. Both beds were made and there were no clothes lying all on the floor as usual. Even though they weren't hanging neatly, it was rather well for a first.

Around four o'clock, the house was full of relatives, namely the little cousins and their mother.

Gomes had left after lunch. He hadn't been seen ever since. They were happy: they couldn't stand the sight of him anymore. One of the lodgers next door called Tony over the wall and gave him an adventure book. He was embarrassed, but also touched by the gift.

He invited him in, but he refused with a smile. He wanted to enjoy the beach!

Bea and Chris felt uncomfortable. They had no gift for their cousin. The punishment had kept them from leaving the house the day before. If only they had known beforehand! Chris ended up giving the birthday boy a golden pen. Though he had had it for a couple of years, it was brand new.

"Thank you, Chris. You didn't have to. You didn't know it was my birthday," Tony said, accepting the gift, confused.

"I'm delighted to give it to you!"

Bea went outside. She was annoyed. She had no gift for her cousin. She had grown quite fond of him. He had never scolded her as Daniel did whenever he had the chance, and he wasn't always messing with her like Chris. He was her favorite cousin by far.

Suddenly, she had a great idea. Even her eyes laughed. Ah, there was a nice gift to give to Tony! He would be delighted!

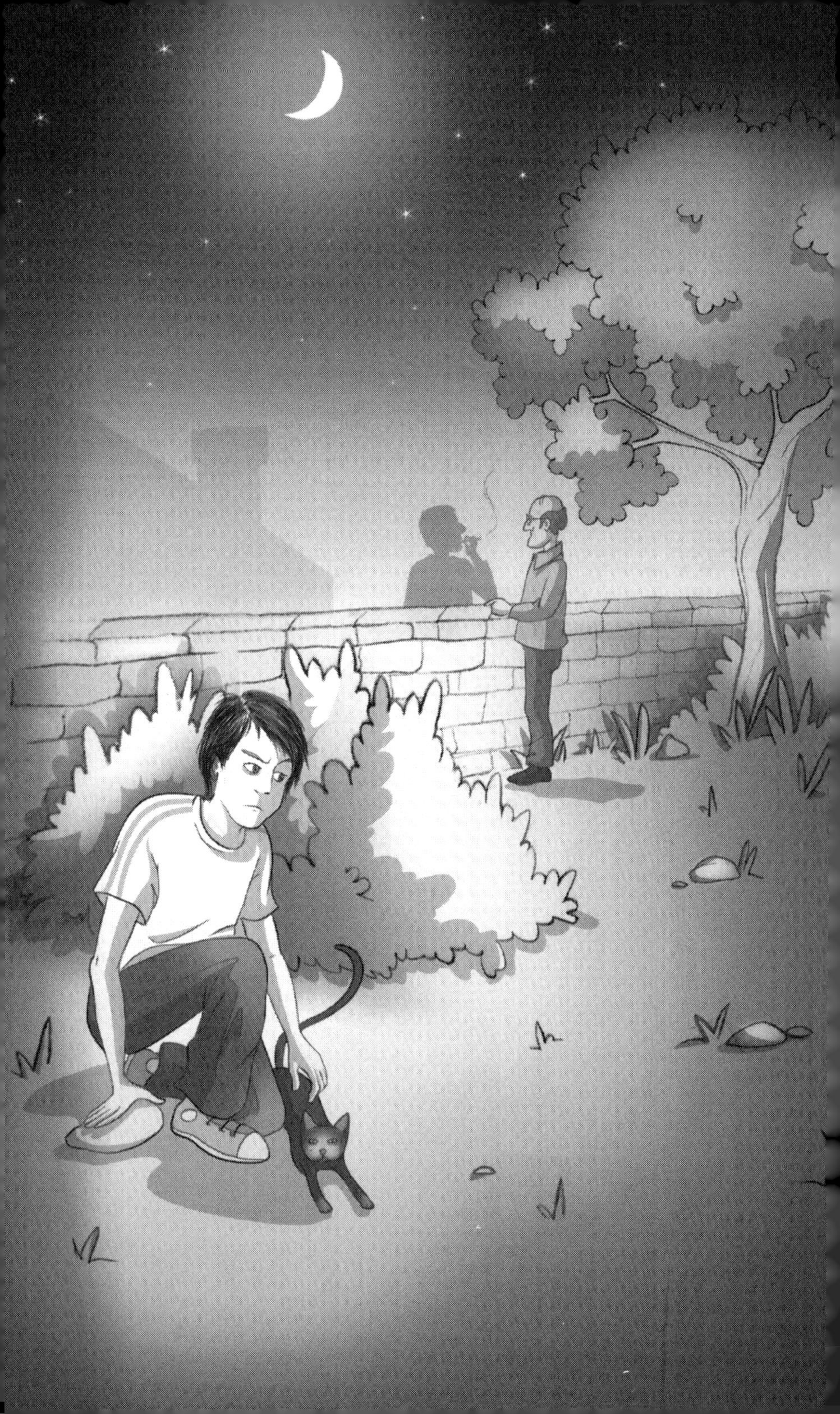

Chapter 14

On their way to adventure!

To everyone's amazement, Bea entered the room pushing her bike.

"This is my gift to you, Tony. I hope you don't mind it's not brand new," she said with a broad smile. "Happy birthday!"

«Happy birthday! Happy birthday! Well, whaddya know?» Jack said, then laughed out loud. Everyone laughed.

Tony looked at her, dumbfounded. He couldn't believe what he had heard. He had wanted so much to have a bike like theirs. Not only was it the latest model, but it also was extremely light compared to his old bike. He was so excited he didn't say a word for a moment.

Daniel just gaped. His mother touched his chin, laughing.

"Thank you, Bea. You're very generous! But now you don't have a bike!"

She laughed. "Don't worry. My birthday's at Christmastime. I'll get another one as a gift, you'll see! I'll ride yours if I need to!"

And that was how it was. Though Tony liked his cousin very much, what she did made him like her even more. He had received many gifts from his parents, his brother, and the rest of the family, but that was the one he liked most.

Something else was in store for him that day. When they were all in the living room celebrating, a well-known figure came in, looking embarrassed. The lodger from the house next door, whom the children hated, was holding a present in his hand. He walked into the room uninvited and greeted the boy with a handshake.

"I wish you a happy birthday! I hope you like this modest gift," he said, smiling.

Somewhat astonished, Tony took the present. He didn't know what to say or do. No matter how hard he tried, he could not bring himself to like him. Besides, he was convinced that he was in it together with Gomes to get the mysterious CD. He looked at the others for help, but they were as dumbstruck as he was. The gift was still in his hands. He didn't know whether he should accept it or not. He didn't want to be rude and turn it down.

"Come on! Open it! See if you like it! I hope you do. I'm not really sure what boys your age like. Unfortunately, I never had children! I've always been very sick, you know! You have no idea what my life's been like: I've been sick all the time. You wouldn't believe it!" he lamented in a plaintive voice, looking at the two sisters. The youngest was staring at him, astonished. She hadn't met him before. Her nephews and godchildren had not told her anything about him yet.

"Have some sweet rice, Mr. Cruz! It's very good. My mother made it!" Christine said, with a smile.

He shook his head, looking sad. "Thank you, but I can't. I'm allergic to cinnamon, you see? You have no idea what my life is like."

"Then, have something else. A little slice of cake. Do stay! We'll sing «Happy Birthday» and cut the cake in a moment!" Tony's grandmother said.

"I suppose I can stay a little longer. You're such a nice family! So, aren't you going to open it?"

The boy shuddered in embarrassment. He tore up the package. The crazy idea that there might be a bomb inside crossed his mind. He laughed at himself.

There was a box and, inside, there were small yet powerful binoculars—quite good ones, too. He was speechless. Only a few moments later did he manage to mumble thank you.

Everyone praised the gift. Mr. Cruz was extremely proud. He started showing him how the binoculars work. The boy was even more confused.

"This guy's in it together with Mr. Gomes, Godmom. We found it out yesterday," Daniel whispered in her ear.

"None of us likes him. How dare he, making himself invited! All the better to spy on us, I'm sure," Bea observed, softly.

"You children have fun. I'll be watching him. Don't worry," their godmother said, looking at the man out of the corner of her eye. She understood why they didn't like him. They were completely right. He looked disgusting! He looked like he hadn't washed his hair in ages.

She stayed close to him all the time. When they closed the blinds to light the candles on the cake and sing «Happy Birthday», she noticed he had turned his back on them and seemed to be doing something on the table. She came close to him, curious. Her eyes widened, astonished, when she realized what he had been doing. She gave him a strange look. He stared at her intently, too. They seemed to probe each other: he was wry; she was perplexed.

The lights came on. The four of them noticed their strange look for a few seconds, then hurried towards Christine, who was cutting and handing out slices of the delicious-looking cake.

No one had dinner that evening. They had feasted on the most delicious sweets. They only had a glass of milk before going to bed. Of course, Daniel ate a generous slice of pudding. He wouldn't have been able to sleep if he hadn't.

"You shouldn't have more, you know? You keep sticking your finger in it," his mother said.

Daniel looked at her indignantly.

"I didn't do it! Not this time! It must have been one of the others. I always take the blame!"

"There, there! It's ok. Now, go to bed, all of you. You look like you could do with a good night's sleep. Don't say a word, Tony! I know what you're going to say. You told me about a dozen times already! You need a good snack to spend the whole day at the beach tomorrow. I heard it the first time. Rest assured! Now, move!" their mother said, exasperated. She was still doing the washing-up after the party and there was little patience left.

The phone rang. Tony, who was close by, answered. His countenance became concerned little by little. He hung up and called the others. They ran up the stairs, entered one of the rooms and closed the door behind them.

"That was Zaza. When she got home, the place was thrashed. Everything was searched. You can imagine what they were looking for!"

"So? Did they find it?"

Tony laughed.

"Whoever it was, they left empty-handed. The CD is well hidden. Still, before she hung up, Zaza said something else—something a bit strange..."

"What was it?" they all asked at the same time, looking at him, full of curiosity.

"She told me not to worry about the guy next door. She says he's harmless. I'm sure Gomes did all the dirty work!"

"I have an idea! Gomes has no cell phone now, so he only talks to his partner at night. What if one of us hid in the garden, waiting for him to meet the idiot next door?" Daniel said. His eyes were shining with excitement. "I can do it. I'm small. I can hide without being seen. So, what do you say?"

The others were silent for a few seconds. Then they agreed. It was a beautiful idea. They only regretted they had not had such a brilliant plan. The three of them stood by the window. They saw Daniel go out and hide behind a small bush, a little away from the wall. He was convinced he would be able to hear everything perfectly there without being seen. Besides, there was no full moon.

Time went by. Nothing happened. The three ended up lying down. They could no longer stand. They were sleepy and very tired. It had been a long day. They were happy they weren't the ones crouching behind a bush for hours on end, waiting for something that might not even happen.

Daniel was thinking something along the same line. He was beginning to feel sorry for himself when he heard a noise close by. Cautious footsteps stopped near the wall. He realized someone had lit a cigarette. He waited. His heart was pounding. It beat with such fury he wondered if the man could hear it.

A few moments later, he heard footsteps on the other side of the wall and pricked up his ears, trying to listen to the whole conversation.

"So? Do you have it?"

"No. I looked everywhere. I couldn't find it. It must be very well hidden!"

"You moron! Maybe you weren't looking in the right place. What's the best place to hide a CD? The computer! Did you look there, at least?"

"Of course I did, Cruz! Do you think I'm stupid? It was the first place I looked. I tried all the CDs I found. Nothing! Then I remembered to search the computer. It was really hard to find the files. I looked into what their aunt has been working on lately, but I ended up giving up. It was so boring I almost fell asleep! These people can themselves writers! I could do much better!"

"You fool! She writes children's stories. They're everything but boring, at that! That's what she wants you to think. There must be a backup copy somewhere. Anyway, you can't go back now. If she's as suspicious as those brats are, she probably wiped out everything from her computer. All we can do is find the CD. It must be very well hidden, though. I have a feeling we'll never find it!"

Daniel was perfectly still, trying to commit everything he heard to memory. Suddenly, he nearly screamed. Something had brushed his legs. Stone cold, he flinched. He felt his heart was about to explode.

He realized what had happened. The next-door neighbor's cat had brushed his legs, delighted to find company behind the bush. It meowed, satisfied.

The men stood silent.

"What was that?!"

"It sounded like a cat. It must be from around here. Forget it!"

Daniel couldn't listen to most of the conversation from then on. The cat kept meowing right next to his ears, showing how happy it was. All he could hear were a few words here and there. He was looking forward to getting back to his comfy bed. He had been crouching there for so long he was feeling numb. Those guys just kept yapping! To think that some people say women talk too much!

A few minutes later, he stopped hearing voices. He realized Gomes had gone inside. He waited a few moments and peeked. He shooed the cat off. The cat was outraged. It had been keeping him company for so long! The nerve of him!

Daniel came out of the bush. It was hard for him to straighten up for a moment. He had been still for too long. Finally, he managed to do it and silently tried to open the door. To his surprise, it was locked! Just his luck!

He started to mumble under his breath. He called all the names he knew to whoever was to blame for his predicament. He couldn't sleep outside. He had to try to wake the others up. How would he be able to do it without drawing the enemy's attention to himself?

He saw the light in Gomes's room go on and waited impatiently for him to turn it off. It didn't happen. Apparently, Gomes was not sleepy. Furious, he kicked the grass, then looked for something to throw at his bedroom window.

He found two pebbles. He aimed and threw one of them. Unfortunately, it hit the wall of his cousins' room, causing a huge racket in the dead of night—at least, it sounded like that. He hid behind the bush when he saw the light in the lodger's room going on again.

Gomes's head popped out of the window. He was curious.

"Meow! MEOW!" Daniel went, mimicking the cat as best he could.

"Stupid cat!"

Gomes went back inside and closed the window.

Daniel smiled mockingly. If he were seeing the lighter side of the situation, he would have meowed some more, just to annoy him. He threw the other stone. This time it hit the target. He patiently waited for his brother to come to the window. He didn't. He was sound asleep.

A disheveled head appeared at the next window.

"Bea! Can you open the door, please?"

She went down silently, turned the key, let him in, then locked the door behind her. They went up to Daniel's room, trying not to draw the attention of the man in the next room.

"I'll wake up Chris. We'll meet you back in your room!"

Daniel came in. He shook his brother, to no avail. He muttered under his breath and decided to tickle his feet. Tony laughed. Daniel covered his mouth.

"Hey! What are you doing? Stop it! Are you crazy?"

"Shut up! I thought you'd never wake up! I threw tons of pebbles at your window and nothing happened. It was Bea who opened the door for me. That good-for-nothing Gomes locked me out," whispered Daniel, sitting on his bunk. "Bea and Chris will meet us here. Have I got news for you!"

Tony sat up, fully awake. When their cousins came in, they sat down, too, listening anxiously. Jack was also there. He looked as interested as they were.

"I couldn't hear much afterwards because of that noisy cat. I heard one of them say boys, compel, unveil, CD. I don't remember anything else."

"Anyway, you managed to listen to lots of stuff. Now we're sure that Gomes and Abel Cruz are in this together, because you heard him calling his name. Zaza was wrong."

"We should get some sleep. Otherwise, we won't be able to wake up early," Chris reminded them, yawning loudly. Of course, they did the same.

Jack mimicked his yawning. He couldn't be silent any longer.

The four children went to their beds. They dreamed of caves, cats and men whispering in the corners, as well as having sweets and a lot of *Molotof* pudding.

Daniel was the first to wake up. He jumped out of bed, excited, in anticipation of they had planned to do that day. He hurried to wake the others up. Soon they went downstairs in silence, so as not to wake Gomes.

The smell of fresh bread and fried meat whetted everyone's appetite. Christine had prepared a snack that would feed an army. They wondered if they could carry all that food on their back. There were steak sandwiches and cheese sandwiches, slices of chocolate cake and orange cake, packs of juice, water bottles, boiled eggs, fruit, toffees, patties, and croquettes. Everything looked delicious. They kissed her and greeted her. They were feeling fine—so fine they could even kiss disgusting-looking Cruz.

"I'm not sure this is a good day to go to the beach, but you know best. The sun isn't out yet and it's windy. I hope your Dad doesn't go overboard today. Watch out for the color of the flags! Don't mess around with the sea!"

They nodded and continued to eat. They had agreed not to

tell her they were going to Praia do Norte. She might forbid them to do it. That just wouldn't do.

"Have you seen my old sneakers, Aunt Christine?" Bea asked, swallowing a piece of bread so fast she nearly choked. "I'd like to wear them. I don't want to get the new ones dirty."

"I washed them. Now, where did I put them?" she wondered, tapping her forefinger thoughtfully. Not matter how hard she tried she couldn't bring herself to remember.

"Perhaps you put them in the trash," Daniel suggested maliciously.

Bea's eyes widened, astonished. Her brother smiled.

"Of course not! I'm not that absentminded!" his mother replied, indignant. She opened the cupboard, then the laundry basket. Nothing. She even peeked into the trash can.

The four children took pity on her and started to look for them, too, giggling. It was Tony who found them in the freezer. They all looked at each other, astonished, then they burst out laughing. They couldn't help it. Their mother laughed even more than they did.

"Well, one thing's for sure: they'd never go bad!" Tony said mockingly.

Bea put on her shoes. She was so amused tears were running down her face.

They stuffed everything into their backpacks as best they could, said goodbye and hopped on their bikes. Tony was riding the one that had been given to him as a gift and Bea was riding his cousin's bike.

They were happy and excited. At long last, they were on their way to adventure! What a thrill just to say that word: ADVENTURE!

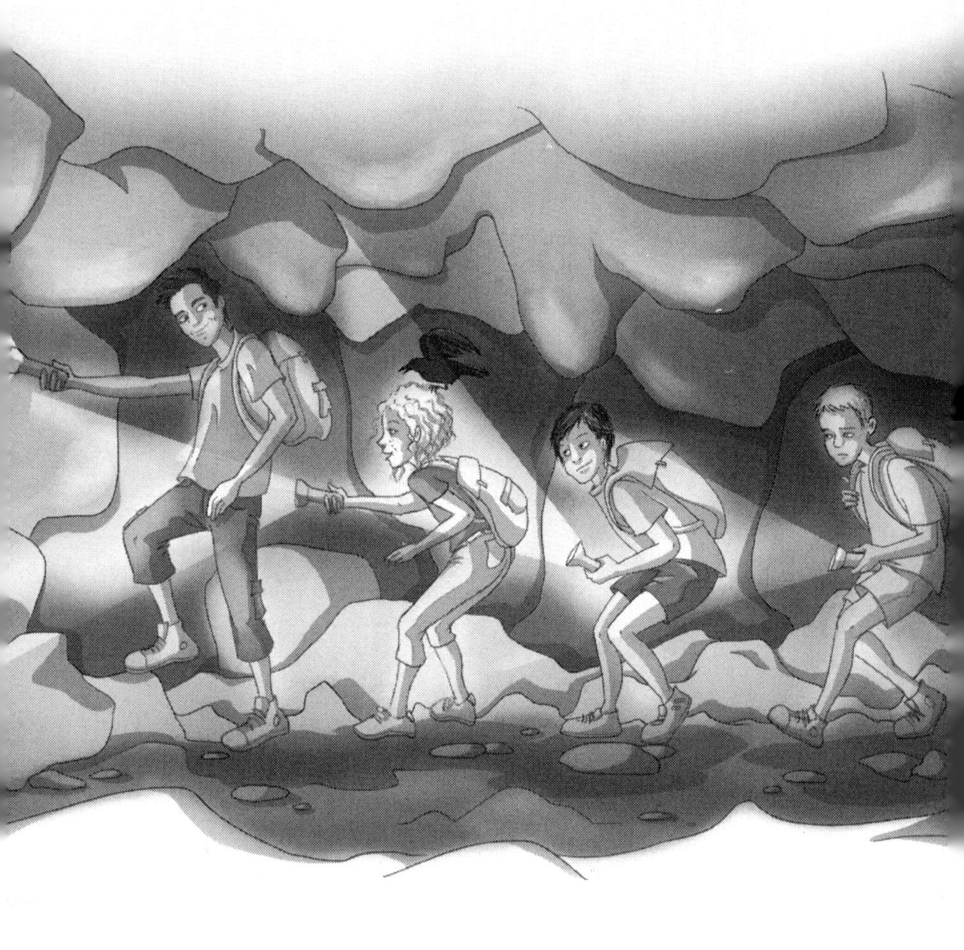

Chapter 15

Deep inside the *suberco*

They cycled to the fort, parked their bikes and ran down the path. Food was wobbling inside their backpacks, bumping into water bottles and packs of juice. To their great satisfaction, the beach was deserted because of the fog and the terrible wind. This was not a good day to go the beach.

"Have you all brought your flashlights?" Tony asked.

"Yes, boss! And spare batteries, just in case," Bea replied cheerfully.

"Good! It would be no fun to find ourselves in the dark in there. We might fall down a hole."

"I also brought a strong rope from your garage in case we need it. I hope we don't!" Chris said, lifting his t-shirt and showing the rope wrapped around his waist. It made him look strange. The others laughed.

"I knew there was something going on! Suddenly, you looked very fat," Daniel said, laughing. The crow mimicked him.

«Naughty boy! Rascal!»

"You're it, you crazy bird!"

Jack pulled his owner's hair. «Crazy bird! Rascal! Naughty boy!»

They took off their shoes, jumped onto the sand, then ran along the beach, laughing at all the nonsense the crow said.

They stopped when they got close to the opening to the cave. The waves still crashed there from time to time. They sat down in a circle.

"We better wait a little longer. We don't need to get wet before we go inside," Chris said, looking at his watch.

"We can chat while we wait."

And so they did. Time flew. They got up, ran towards the rocks, and sat on them to put on their shoes. They tied the towels to their backpacks and looked at each other, eyes shining.

"Shall we?" Tony asked by the entrance.

"LET'S GO!" everyone replied.

«Let's go! Well, whaddya know?» Jack said, taking flight from his owner's shoulder when he saw she was getting ready to enter that smelly hole. He uttered indignant screams but decided to join her when he saw she was going in anyway. He muttered something no one understood, but which was surely meant to show his complete disapproval for such an expedition.

Tony got in, followed by Bea and Jack, Daniel and finally Chris. They were holding their flashlights and pointing them everywhere.

"Aren't we going to explore this cave?" Daniel asked, pointing to the round-shaped opening in the ground and watching the sand glowing down there.

Tony and Bea, who by now were crouching on the rocks, stopped and turned to him. Chris was still at the entrance.

"How do we go down?"

"We could tie the rope to that rock. It looks very solid to me!" Tony said, going down behind his cousin. "Give me a hand, Chris! Here! I think it's pretty tight now."

Daniel turned to them. "Don't you find it strange that it's not full of water?"

"It's probably flooded in the winter when the sea is very rough. The opening through which we came in isn't close to the sand, so the sea level must be below the ground in the cave."

"Can I go down first?" Bea asked.

The boys looked at each other, sharing the same thought. If they said no, she might throw them into the hole, remove the rope and leave them there.

"Yes, but then we'll follow you by the same order in which we came in. Take this scarf and tie it on your hand, so your other hand won't be skinned."

Bea took the scarf and clung to the rope. She was so thrilled she felt like screaming and jumping up and down. She went down slowly, holding the flashlight between her teeth and peeking down from time to time. The boys, on their knees, pointed the flashlights down to the bottom so she could see. They were eager to follow her lead. They saw her approach the sand quickly.

"I'm here!" she announced in a slightly muffled voice.

She jumped to the floor, pointing her flashlight up. She saw three excited faces. Jack was still silent. He didn't enjoy the descent at all. He had clung to his owner's head looking like he was afraid he might fall, as if he had forgotten he knew how to fly.

The others came down quickly. When they were beside her, they looked around. They had a funny feeling in their stomach. It was strange to know they were under the sea, listening to it over their heads, ceaselessly roaring. Chris shivered at the thought of the sea breaking in, drowning them. Still, he didn't say a word, ashamed of his fear. The sand under their feet was damp and there were a few pebbles scattered around. They shone every time the flashlights beamed on them. The walls and the ceiling were made of rock. The cave wasn't very large, though it was big enough for the four of them.

"I wonder if there's a way out," Tony said, pointing the flashlight around. The cave narrowed ahead.

They took a step in that direction, curious.

"It seems so. Look! It looks like it goes down!"

"Let's see where it will lead!" the intrepid Bea said, looking anxiously at the others. Her younger cousin agreed.

Chris shook his head disapprovingly. "I don't think it's a good idea. We should have another rope, in case one of us happens to slip. It must be very slippery down there. We mustn't take chances!"

Tony agreed, much to the younger ones' disappointment.

"Leave it for some other time. Now let's go up!"

One by one, they made their way up. It was much harder now than when they went down, of course. They were tired. They stopped to get their strength back. They resumed after Chris wrapped the rope around his waist again.

They crouched on stones piled on top of one another. They didn't speak. They needed to concentrate so they wouldn't slip. They felt they were curving to the left. After some time, they seemed to go straight ahead. They stood up, pointing their flashlights to the rock walls. There was a stale smell in the air, but they slowly got used to it and didn't even notice a few minutes later. The ground was now sort of flat, although they still stumbled from time to time. They were going along a passage that was wide enough for two people to walk side by side. It meandered here and there. After what seemed like ages, they went into a strange-shaped cave: it was neither round nor square, oval, or rectangular. The walls were made of pebbles that looked as if they had gathered at random. The ground was partly covered by very white sand.

"Have you seen this? The sea must reach this cave in the winter!" Tony said.

"Maybe we'll find a cave with stalactites and stalagmites. That would be awesome!" Bea said, excited.

"I don't think we will. Usually that only happens where there's limestone. This rock looks very different. Did you notice, when we went down from the fort to Praia do Norte, that the ground was red, and the rocks seemed to be made of pebbles all clinging to each other?" Chris recalled. "Just like this."

"What's stala—whatever?"

"Stalactites. They're formations that hang from the ceiling of some caves. Stalagmites are those that are formed on the ground."

"Oh, I know what you're talking about! I've seen it on television. What a pity there's none of those here!"

They walked around, trying to find a way out. They were beginning to feel discouraged when the little girl found a narrow, half-hidden opening.

"Come on! This way!" she announced, shining the flashlight on Tony's face, waiting for him to step ahead of her.

"Be careful. There may be a hole like the one that swallowed the dog, the shepherd, and the priest around here. That would be no fun at all!"

They all shivered when they pictured the scene.

"If that happens, you'll be the first to fall, dumdum. You're leading. You're the one who should be really careful, otherwise we'll fall right behind you!" Daniel replied, trying to laugh without succeeding. He pointed the flashlight to the crow. "Have you noticed Jack hasn't said a word in a while, Bea?"

His cousin smiled, patting the crow. "He doesn't like our expedition at all. Jack prefers to be out in the open!"

Chris understood him well. He felt the same way. He seemed to be the least adventurous of the four. The tunnel became increasingly narrow, so they had to crouch. They began to fear it would become too narrow for them. It didn't, much to their relief. They ended up in a cave that was smaller than the previous one. It was made of smooth rock and there were no pebbles on the walls. The ceiling was higher, allowing them to walk upright.

"I don't know about you guys, but I'm starving!" Tony confessed, rubbing his belly. "I refuse to walk further before I grab something to eat."

The others laughed and agreed. They were hungry, too. Walking had whetted their appetite, which was usually quite large anyway. They sat on the rock ground and unzipped their backpacks, mouths watering at the sight of so much good food. Jack was delighted when he realized the children were about to have a snack. Now that was a good idea! He totally agreed.

They unwrapped meat sandwiches soaked in a delicious gravy. They tasted great! They washed them down with some pineapple juice. The crow ate a lot, too: everyone gave him bits of food. They put the empty packages in a bag and left them in a corner. They'd take them out on the way back.

"Get up, you lazy girl! We don't have all day!" Chris said.

«Lazy girl! Naughty boy! Well, whaddya know?»

The four laughed, happy he had spoken again.

They had to crouch for some time.

"This seems to go on forever!" Tony observed, pointing the flashlight to the ceiling. He stopped for a few seconds. His cousin bumped into him, and subsequently the others bumped into her.

"You better tell me the next time you decide to stop. You scared me!" Bea said, chuckling.

They resumed. The path was now high enough for an adult to walk upright. They had a feeling they had been walking for ages. The underground path seemed endless. Fortunately, they had their flashlights to light their way. Walking around in the dark down there stumbling on rocks would be no walk in the park.

"It seems we're going up. Do you think this will lead to the cave where the Image of Our Lady of Nazaré was for all those years?" Daniel asked. He was thrilled at the idea that they might suddenly appear in the chapel, to everyone's amazement. If anyone saw several people coming out from behind the bars, they would get quite a scare, or maybe faint. Perhaps they'd think they were seeing ghosts. It would be so cool! he couldn't help thinking.

He was right. They kept going up. It seemed the path was endless. Suddenly, they stopped.

"What's wrong?"

"Why did you stop?"

"Are we there yet?"

"That's not it. There are two different tunnels: one goes ahead and the other turns to the right. Which one do you think we should take?" Tony asked, undecided.

"I say let's stick to this one! What do you say?" Chris asked.

"I think so, too. We'll explore the other one later!"

"Let's find out where this one goes first. I'm sure it goes all the way up to the chapel! These must be the underground tunnels mentioned in the book and in the piece of wood below the crucifix! They have to be!" Daniel said. He was getting more and more excited.

"So, the only way is up!"

They went on, tirelessly. The ground became increasingly uneven. Rocks were huddled together, which sometimes made their way difficult. It never crossed their minds to give up and go back, of course. They found themselves in a high-ceilinged cave. It was larger than the ones they had seen before. They walked around, exploring. Suddenly, a desperate scream made their hair stand on end. They continued to hear it, though it was very muffled. They pointed their flashlights to one another, frightened. Jack let out distressing squeaks, as if he were wounded to death, which made them even more terrified.

"Where's Bea?" Tony asked anxiously. The others looked at him, their hearts sinking. They pointed their flashlights around and saw the crow flying.

"Idiot! There's nothing wrong with you!" Chris scolded him.

"Leave him alone, Chris! The poor thing must be as scared as we are!" Daniel said, a little annoyed.

"Bea! BEA! Where are you?"

«BEA! BEA! BEA!» Jack seemed more frightened than the boys.

"Down here! I fell down a hole! I can't see anything. I lost my flashlight. There's a weird pungent smell here."

The boys pointed their flashlights to the ground cautiously, afraid they might fall, too. The light beamed on the little girl. She was dirty and was rubbing her arms and legs as she looked up, blinking. The hole was quite deep. Their eyes widened as they watched everything closely. Two human skeletons were right beside her. A smaller one, an animal, was by her feet.

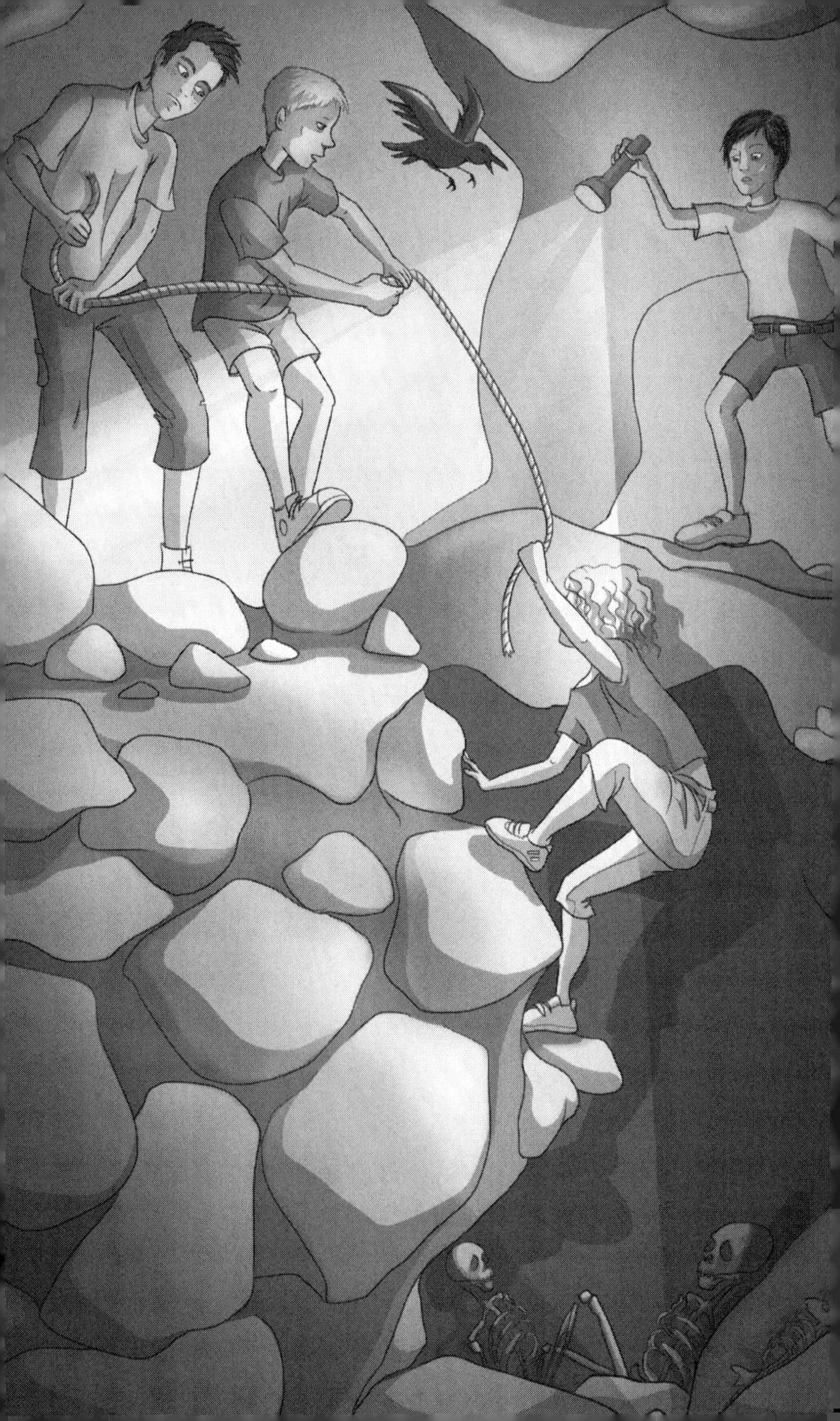

Chapter 16

Trapped underground!

"Bea! Are you okay?" Chris asked. His voice was shaking. "You have nothing broken?"

"I don't think so. Just a few scratches and bruises," she said, checking herself. She looked around as she saw the shock in their countenance. She shuddered and gasped when she saw her unique company. When she spoke again, her voice didn't seem to belong to her. "These must be the unfortunate people who fell down here all those years ago. That must be the skeleton of the dog that disappeared. Poor people! They must have died a horrible death, with no one to help them!"

"Take it easy. We'll get you out in no time! Give me the rope, Chris!" Tony asked, afraid she might start screaming. She didn't. The three boys earned a new respect for her.

Chris untied the rope. His hands were shaking. He threw it down the hole, holding it steadily with the help of his older cousin. Daniel silently pointed the light down so that his cousin could see the rope.

They pulled Bea up, while she helped using her hands and her feet. She didn't even complain about the scratches on her legs. Once she was back up safe and sound, they hugged her, relieved, unable to utter a word. The crow clung to his owner's shoulder, rubbing his beak on her face, and whispering nonsense in her ear with a tender-looking gaze.

"It was a miracle you didn't break a leg or an arm," Daniel said. He was finally able to speak again.

She tried to smile. She looked very pale, despite all the dirt on her face. "That's true. I was very lucky! Dear Jack! I must have given you quite a scare!"

"Your rope sure came in handy, Chris! It was a great idea!" Tony praised him, patting his shoulder.

Chris smiled, pleased. It was the first time his cousin praised him. After so much criticism, it felt good to be praised.

They had some water. They were tired after all the effort. Then they looked for the lost flashlight. They found it.

"Fortunately, it still works!" Bea said, trying it out. She pointed it to the hole. "Wow! That's deep!"

«Wow! That's deep! Well, whaddya know?» Jack said. He finished with a big sneeze—perhaps it was for real, perhaps it wasn't. They were startled.

"Stop saying all that nonsense, you fool! We'll be scared to death!" Chris scolded him disapprovingly.

«Nonsense! Nonsense, you fool! Well, whaddya know?»

The four children laughed, amused. That crow was the worst!

"Let's go this way. Be careful not to slip!"

They climbed some steps roughly carved in the rock, treading them carefully, afraid they might crumble under their feet. They had been there for centuries.

"Do you think Friar Romano made these steps?" Daniel asked. His voice was full of emotion.

"Most likely," Chris replied. He was moved as well.

The ceiling was getting higher. The walls were made of big rocks piled up. They came across a chamber with a very uneven ground. They pointed their flashlights around.

"Let's hope there aren't any bats around here," Tony said.

"Bats?!"

"Yes. Bats have been spotted on the rocks of the *suberco*. I don't know whether that's true or not. I hope it isn't."

Daniel and Bea gasped. That part of the adventure would be very unpleasant if they found any bats. They walked on cautiously, then stopped when they heard Bea's terrified cry again.

"Something got stuck to my face and my hair! Help me!"

The boys beamed their flashlights on her face and smiled.

"It's just cobwebs. Maybe hundreds of years old," Chris said, laughing.

She bit her lip. For someone who hadn't screamed when she saw skeletons, screaming like that over cobwebs was such a shame!

"Sorry. It was very stupid of me."

"Come on, Bea. It's ok! We were talking about bats anyway. It's only natural you were scared," Tony said, patting her.

His cousin looked at him gratefully, determined not to scream even if she was attacked by a dozen bats.

They walked on the stones. The crow stayed very close to his owner and didn't even dare to squeak. He found the outing was very long and unpleasant. What were those kids thinking, strolling along in dark, smelly places like that?

They ended up in another chamber, which was roughly the same size as the previous one. Tony, who was the first to enter, stumbled and nearly fell. He pointed the flashlight to the ground, curious.

"This is it! Look at the candles! We're standing right under the chapel!" Tony exclaimed, excited.

"It's so dark in here! Can you believe it? We did it!" Bea exclaimed, her eyes shining like stars. He peered through the wire mesh and the bars, pointing his flashlight out.

"Let's scare anyone who comes down here!" Daniel suggested with a mischievous smile.

They laughed. If anyone saw them standing behind the padlocked bars, they'd be frightened.

"Better not. We might give them a heart attack. We should go back the way we came," Chris advised, softly pushing aside cobwebs that had lovingly clung to his hair.

"But then no one will ever know we were here!" Daniel said indignantly. "How will anyone believe us? They'll say we're lying when we tell them we've been here. We must let everyone know we discovered the caves, otherwise what's the point?"

«Nonsense, you fool! Nonsense!» Jack said, straight to the point as usual. They laughed.

Daniel stared at him dumbfounded, convinced Jack had really understood their conversation. He looked at the crow, amazed.

"Can you imagine what adults will say to us if they see us here and realize all the danger we've been through? They'll skin us alive! Mom will be the first in line! We'll be grounded for the rest of our lives! Is that what you want, Daniel?"

Daniel was staring at his brother, looking a bit sad.

"Of course not. But you must agree it's very boring not to be able to tell anyone!"

«Well, whaddya know? Nonsense!»

They laughed again. The crow started coughing, then sneezed hard twice. It sounded very strange underground. He stopped, scared.

"Serves you right, Jack! Stop showing off, will you?" Chris scolded him.

«Naughty boy! Rascal! Nonsense, you fool!»

"Well, we better get back, before our laughter destroys this place. How about a snack? I'm so hungry right now!" Tony said, with a little laugh.

"I'm hungry, too, but I'd rather eat somewhere else. There are too many cobwebs here for my taste," Bea confessed, following her cousin.

"Let's eat in the other cave. Come on!"

Suddenly, Tony stopped, forcing them to stop, too. He turned to them.

"You know what? We forgot all about the time. We were so excited we didn't even notice the time. It's almost six o'clock. No wonder we're so hungry!"

For a moment they were silent, staring at the clock. They were all thinking the same, but they didn't dare say it out loud.

Time had gone by so quickly. The tide had probably covered the entrance to the cave by then.

"Maybe we should save our snack for later and get on the way," Chris said, with a nervous laugh. He looked at the others, hoping they'd agree.

"You're right, Chris. Let's do it. We can explore the other path tomorrow!"

They all agreed. They walked as fast as they could, without even realizing it. They avoided the treacherous hole cautiously and resumed the underground path.

They passed the cave where they had a snack and headed for the pebble cave. When they were getting to the entrance to the passage, a deafening noise made them stop. They looked at each other, frightened.

"What was that?" Daniel asked in a hushed voice.

"It must be the sea hitting against the rocks," Chris replied.

"In that case..."

"We're trapped, at least until the tide goes down again," Tony concluded, very serious.

They stared at each other in the light of the flashlights. They were very pale. They couldn't utter a single word. They all knew the situation was very serious.

"Mom'll be worried sick, Tony!"

The boy bit his lip, angry at himself. He shouldn't have forgotten such an important detail as the tide timetable. Now they were all trapped underground because of him. There was no way out.

"I have an idea. It seems to me I'm the one who can hold his breath longer here. I'll make my way through the passage as best as I can and then go out and seek help."

Bea shuddered. She became even paler. She grabbed his arm. "OH, NO YOU WON'T! The sea would hurl you against the rocks! It would tear you to pieces. Please don't! The sea's really rough here!"

She was so terrified he hugged her awkwardly.

"If it scares you so much, then I won't. We'll wait together until the tide goes down again. It'll just take a few hours. Time will go by in a flash."

"Will we be able to breathe well? After all, the passage is full of water," Daniel recalled, with a shiver.

They shuddered.

"We should go to the chapel cave. Someone may hear us there," Chris suggested hopefully. The idea of spending part of the night trapped underground was not pleasant at all.

Tony shook his head. "Maybe we shouldn't. Chances are it would be closed when we got there. We'd get tired for nothing. Let's wait in the pebble cave. I don't think the sea will reach it. It probably only happens in winter."

The others followed his decision. Deep down they knew that, besides being the oldest, he was the most sensible of them all.

They turned around and went to the pebble cave. They wrapped themselves in the towels and sat down next to each other against the rock, very close together. They had started feeling cold all of a sudden. Jack hopped around, pecking the pebbles, curious.

"Do you guys want to eat?" Bea asked, unzipping her backpack. "I must confess I'm starving."

"Good idea! Time will go by much faster and the whole situation won't seem so unpleasant," Chris said, unzipping his backpack, too.

"You're right. Can you imagine if we had nothing to eat? It would be no fun at all. I'm glad Mom packed so much food! It's like she knew it all along!" Daniel said. He cheered up when he saw so much good food.

"We should leave one flashlight on and turn off the others," Tony suggested, wise as usual.

"I wonder how Aunt Christine is feeling right now. Poor thing! She must be so worried!"

What they didn't know is that she had no idea the children were in trouble. She had gone to Peniche to take some things to her husband, who had headed there when his ship broke down. She had left a note telling her children and her nephews about what had happened so they would not worry about her, suggesting they should have dinner at their sister's when they returned from the beach.

Now they weren't hungry anymore, they leaned against each other, laughing at the foolish things the crow kept saying. Little by little, they fell asleep, exhausted. Only Tony remained awake, thinking about everything that had happened that day. He was the most worried of all. He felt responsible, since he was the oldest. Even though his eyelids insisted on closing, he fought sleep as best he could. He didn't want to get up for fear of waking his cousin, who was leaning against him, sleeping. He smiled as he remembered her face when she saw the skeletons. She really was cool! She didn't start to scream, as you'd expect.

The sound of the waves crashing against the rocks lulled him pleasantly. He fell asleep, tired. The hours passed. They didn't move, although it was far from comfortable there.

Midnight came, then one o'clock, two, three, four, five, six...

Around seven o'clock, Tony woke up with a start, realizing what had happened. The flashlight was very dim. it would go off any minute now. He turned on his flashlight and looked at his watch. He grunted under his breath, annoyed with himself for falling asleep.

"It's no use waking them up and worrying them unnecessarily. I'll wake them up at ten o'clock. We'll have something to eat and then we'll leave. Maybe Mom will put us on bread and water for a month. So be it!"

There was no need to wake them up. Around nine o'clock, the three woke up feeling numb and not knowing where they were.

For a moment they looked around, surprised. Then it all came back to them. They looked at Tony, still sleepy.

"I'm afraid I fell asleep, too. The good news is that it's almost nine o'clock and the tide must be going down," he informed, embarrassed. "Sorry. I know I shouldn't have fallen asleep."

"We were all very tired," Chris admitted, smiling. "Move over, Jack! Go to Bea!"

«Naughty boy! Naughty boy!» the crow said, then laughed. It echoed strangely in the cave. They shuddered.

"Let's eat. I'm starving! It looks like I haven't eaten in ages!" Daniel said, patting the bird.

"Don't you find it odd that there's daylight outside and it's always dark in here?" Bea asked, having a slice of chocolate cake. She gave the crow a nice piece, which he devoured, delighted.

The others silently agreed.

"I've been meaning to ask you something for some time now," Daniel said, looking at Jack, curious. "Who gave you that crow?"

His cousin laughed. "A friend of my Dad's, Mr. Mário. He has lots of birds. You wouldn't believe it! His place rocks! Dad took us there when we were little. There was this crow that looked a lot like Jack—he used to speak too. I went nuts when I saw him! All I wanted was to bring him home!"

"That's right. The only way to drag Bea out of there was to promise her we'd get her one, too. And so it was. We've had it for four years now."

«Nonsense!»

They laughed. They were in a good mood. A few minutes later, they got up, picked up the trash and put it in a bag inside Bea's backpack.

"Shall we go? It's ten o'clock."

"Okay, Daniel. You go first. That's what you want, isn't it?" his brother condescended, smiling.

Daniel gave him a broad smile. He switched on his flashlight and started on his way, followed by Chris, Bea and the crow and Tony.

They walked along the passages, anxious to see daylight again. When they were coming close to the way out, Jack let out a high-pitched cry and flew outside. He was tired of being underground for so long. He burst out screaming.

"What's he saying?" Tony asked, amused.

"The usual nonsense. He's calling everyone he sees scoundrel and naughty boy!" said Bea, chuckling. "He must be ecstatic to be outside." She, too, shared the crow's enthusiasm.

Daniel crossed the opening and slid down the rocks. The others followed, though they were more careful. A beam of artificial light made them blink and shield their eyes with their hands. Curious, they tried to see what caused that light. Their blood froze in their veins at the sound of a voice they knew all too well.

"Well, if it isn't my little friends! You won't believe how happy I am to see you!"

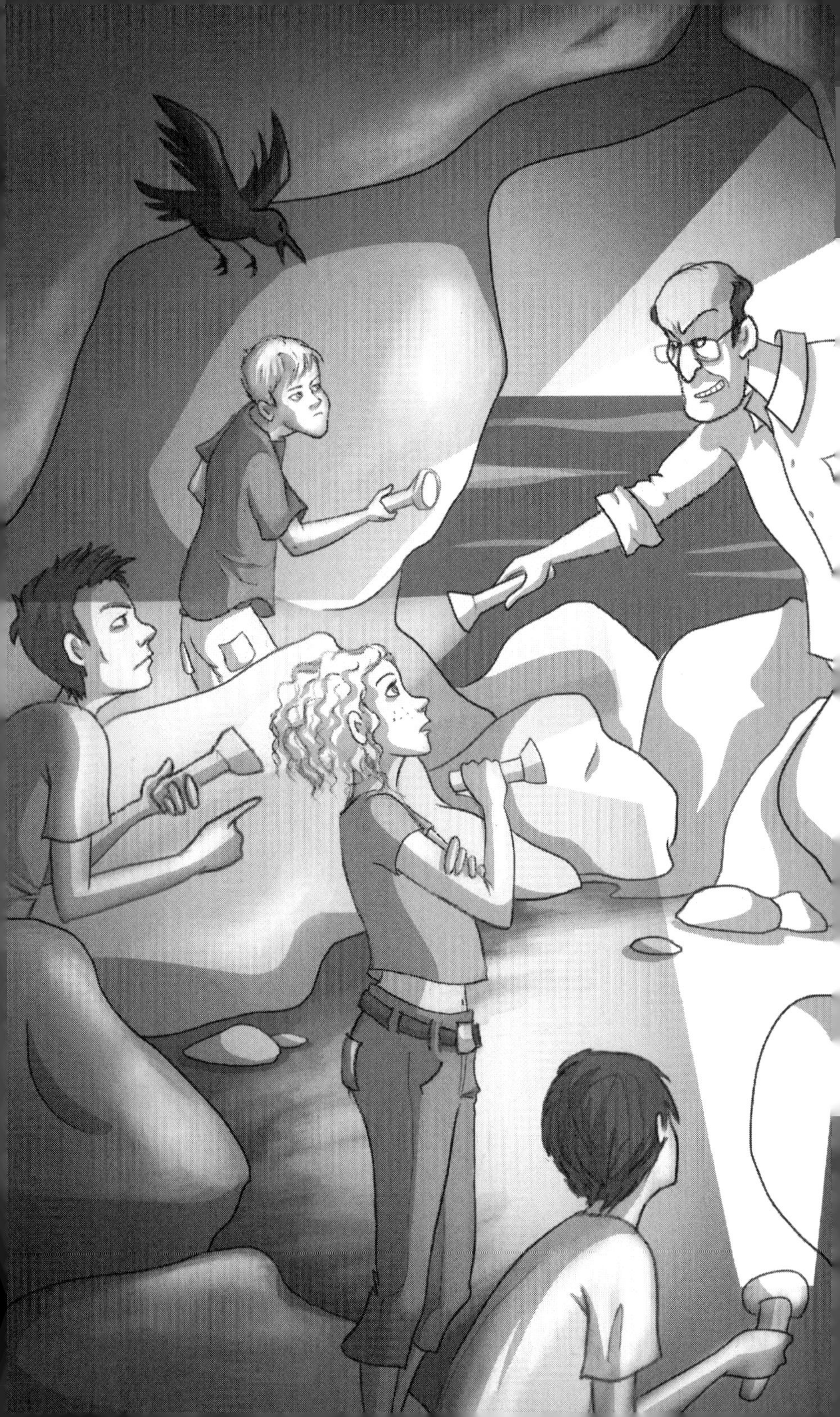

Chapter 17

Prisoners!

They were speechless for a moment, as they realized it was Gomes who inexplicably stood at the entrance to the cave, preventing them from going out to the beach. They pointed their flashlights to him and noticed his menacing look, which was quite different from his usual one when he was in their house. Outside, Jack kept screaming "rascal" and "naughty boy." They felt like hitting themselves for not paying attention to his warnings. It was much too late now! They were in that damned man's hands!

"Let us go, Mr. Gomes! You know you can't keep us here forever!" Tony said, managing his anger.

Gomes chuckled. "Oh, yes, I can!"

"Don't be stupid! What good will it be? Everyone must be looking for us by now. When they learn you tried to stop us from going home, things will not look good for you," Chris threatened coldly.

Gomes laughed again, which made them even angrier. "You have no idea how wrong you are! Right now, your mother doesn't even know about your little outing. She went to Peniche yesterday and hasn't come back yet. This morning she called to ask if everything was okay. I told her you were sleeping like the little angels you are, which was very nice of me, as you'll agree. I didn't want to worry her."

The four children shuddered, realizing he meant it.

"What do you want from us, Mr. Gomes? I don't believe you're still so upset by the little things that happened between us. We've always been so nice to you," Tony said, smiling.

"Don't be stupid, boy! You know perfectly well what I want! You're all smart—unfortunately for you!" he muttered angrily.

They heard a shout outside, and a lot of grumbling.

"What was that, Cruz?"

"The damned crow pecked me! Rascal! He took a piece off my neck!" an irritated voice muttered outside.

The children looked at each other, pleased. Go Jack!

Gomes turned to them. His eyes were flashing. He had realized their satisfaction. "Laugh now. You'll cry later, you fiends!"

"What do you want from us?" Daniel asked rudely. He felt an urge to hurl himself at him.

"You'll learn soon enough. I want one of you to write to your aunt or godmother, or whatever she is to you all, and tell her you are my prisoners and that I will only release you when she hands over the CD your dear dad sent her. If she can get him to come too, which I believe she will, even better! We had planned to kidnap your aunt's brats to force her to give us the CD, but she anticipated it and disappeared with them, so all that's left is you! We'll just have to make do with you."

"How did you find out where we were?" Bea asked, curious.

"I noticed you weren't home yesterday. So, we did a little research around here in the early morning. We found your bikes parked by the fort. Unfortunately, you'll never see them again. Someone might spot them and start thinking. We just couldn't take that chance, could we? By now they're probably smashed against that huge rock in front of the Fort," he told them, sneering when he saw the horror on their faces. "We went down to the beach and, behold, we saw your ill-fated crow mysteriously coming out from an opening in the rocks. Unaware, it did us a great service! It would never occur to me you were here."

Unable to control himself any longer, Daniel hurled himself at him, butting him in the stomach. That was the last straw! Losing his beloved bicycle was more than he could take.

Gomes dropped his flashlight on the floor and punched the boy hard in the ear. Daniel was stunned. When Gomes saw the others were going to attack him, he produced a small weapon, pointing it threateningly with his left hand.

"You'd better not try to test my aim. You may regret it. I'm not kidding!"

The three stepped back, shuddering. They had never seen a real gun before: only in movies on television.

Daniel struggled in his hands, furious, shouting to let him go and trying to kick him in the shins. "Let go of me, you brute! LET GO OF ME!"

"Stop right now, or I'll throw you into that hole in no time, you little savage!" he warned, shaking him so much he was bewildered.

"Leave my brother alone!"

Suddenly, Daniel bit Gomes's hand as hard as he could. Gomes screamed in pain and let him go for a few seconds. Then he threw him into the opening at his feet. Daniel fell helplessly on the bottom of the cave. His whole body sored.

"Let's find out whether you keep your mouth shut or not, you little pest!" Gomes muttered, chuckling.

There was laughter outside. Apparently, the other man had realized what had happened and thought it was funny.

"Get me out of here, you... you dirty stinking scum!"

Gomes opened his eyes wide. He was bewildered. Never before had anyone called him dirty stinking scum. He gasped. He was speechless for a moment. That damn kid! There was no shutting him up!

Despite their dangerous situation, the three cousins could not help smiling when they saw his astonishment. Much to Gomes's fury, a voice outside repeated the same words. He turned very red.

«Dirty stinking scum! Dirty stinking scum! Well, whaddya know? Scoundrel!» Jack shouted, delighted by the sound of the new words and eager to peck the other man, who prevented him from joining his beloved owner, once again. Though he flew right close to him, the other man managed to dodge him, which left him displeased. Why wouldn't he give him the pleasure of letting him peck him?

"SHUT UP!"

"Scoundrel! Dirty stinking scum!" Daniel shouted.

Gomes clenched his fist threateningly. Too bad the boy wasn't close to him: he'd like to punch him hard.

When he realized Tony was rushing towards the enemy, trying to help his brother, Chris grabbed him firmly.

"You, blondie! Come here! Write down what I tell you, if you don't want your little sister to keep that naughty boy company! Cruz, give me the pen and paper, will you?" said Gomes, watching the three children closely to stop them from hurling themselves at him, gun or no gun. A big hand held out what he asked for. "Move, kid! Can't you hear me?"

Chris stared at him, defiant. "No!"

Gomes looked at him threateningly. "If that's what you want, it's your funeral. Don't blame me! Once the tide starts to fill, you can say goodbye to your little cousin. He'll drown. Cool, isn't it? Surely you don't expect me to get him out of there, do you? It must be terrible, watching the sea slowly entering the cave, realizing he's going to drown. I wouldn't like to be in his shoes!" he said, watching them out of the corner of his eye. A sneer came out of his mouth.

The three children shuddered. They were very pale. Fortunately, Daniel didn't understand what Gomes had said. He was still screaming, getting more furious by the minute.

You wouldn't dare!" Tony exclaimed, indignant.

"Are you willing to bet your rude little brother's life?! If you all do as I tell you, I promise I'll get him out of there before the tide comes back up."

Chris ground his teeth. "Where am I supposed to write, anyway? The rocks are wet, and there's nowhere on which to put the piece of paper."

"Take off your backpack and write on it, you idiot! Write down what I told you and don't try anything stupid! Remember I know your names. Don't sign Christopher!"

The boy bit his lip. He was annoyed. Gomes knew what he was thinking. He had thought about doing just that. He sat down on a rock and began to write. His cousin was pointing his flashlight to the piece of paper. He paused for a moment a few times, pondering what to write. He had to come up with a way to let his aunt know, no matter what. He mustn't let her fall into the trap as well, along with his father. It was far too dangerous. God only knew what they would do to him when they had him in their hands.

"Hurry up! It's not like you're writing a novel, you know? Tell her to leave the CD on your doorstep. We'll let you go then. Don't tell her where you are! You'll regret it if you try anything funny!"

The boy stopped writing a few minutes later. He handed him the paper and got up, annoyed.

"Dear Zaza,

We are prisoners of you-know-who. You probably know what they want: the CD. Please give it to them. If possible, tell Dad. Don't tell anyone else. Our lives depend on it. He means it! Daniel's life depends on how quick you act. Gomes promised he'll let us go as soon as he has the CD. Leave it on Aunt Christine's doorstep.

Please pray to your favorite saint, St Romano, for us. Till we meet again!

Love, Chris"

Gomes finished reading, then looked at him mockingly. He held the paper out to the other man, who almost took it from his hands.

"What kind of name is this?! Zaza?!? Is he making a fool of you?" asked a muffled voice on the other side.

"Take it easy, Cruz. That's what the kids call their aunt, or godmother, or whatever!" Gomes replied, turning to the four children. "It seems to me praying to St Romano won't be enough to save that little pest. If your aunt doesn't deliver the CD before the tide rises again, you can kiss Daniel goodbye!"

Chris motioned towards him, indignant.

"You promised you'd get him out of there if I wrote what you wanted!"

"I did? That's funny. I have no recollection of that. You must have got it wrong! If you want to keep your cousin company, just say the word."

"Damn you!" Tony cried. He was even paler than before. You can't leave him there. You don't know if Aunt Christine delivers the CD before the tide fills the cave!"

"You're right. Still, the way I see it, that's not my problem."

The boy clenched his fists. Bea squeezed his hand. She knew what he was feeling. She pulled him back, afraid he'd hurl himself at him, despite the gun. He was so angry he felt his entire body shake.

"You must get him out of there!" Chris shouted, his eyes flashing as he moved towards him.

Gomes twisted Chris's arm behind his back.

"If you're so worried about your little cousin's fate, you don't you keep him company?"

Much to Chris's amazement, he pushed him into the hole.

He landed on top of the astonished Daniel, who was not expecting company at all. Not knowing who had knocked him down, he started to call Gomes the worst names he knew. Gomes ground his teeth, furious.

"If you don't want the same to happen to you, you'd better behave! If there was another way out, you'd have run away through it," he said, chuckling. "I'll just wait right here for the tide to come up. My friend is on his way to deliver the letter. Let's hope the answer will get here in time."

They took Chris's backpack and disappeared into the hole, afraid he might throw them into the hole, too. They walked hand in hand, nervous. They stopped in the pebble cave. They sat on the floor, still shaking.

"What are we going to do, Tony? The tide is about to rise."

"I know, Bea. We have to think of a plan. We can't just leave them there. I don't think we should take the path to the chapel. It's a long way till we get there. Besides, we don't have Chris's rope. We may not have enough time to save them. Perhaps we should wait for Gomes to leave. He will, eventually. I'm sure he will. He's not a fool! He won't risk getting wet."

"So what do you propose to do? What's your plan?"

"We'll wait for the sea to start flooding the cave. Gomes will no longer be there by then. We'll help Daniel and Chris get out before the cave is completely flooded. Then, the four of us will come here. We'll be safe. The only problem is your brother still has the rope."

Bea's eyes shone with enthusiasm.

"Good idea! Chris will throw the rope out here and we'll pull them out!"

"The hardest thing now is to wait."

So they did. They missed the other two. Bea missed Jack very much as well. She missed his company.

Exasperated, they watched time go by very slowly. They were apprehensive. Every once in a while, one of them would check if Gomes was still there. He just wouldn't go away, the scoundrel! They were not enjoying that part of the adventure. They just wished they would all be back outside under the sun!

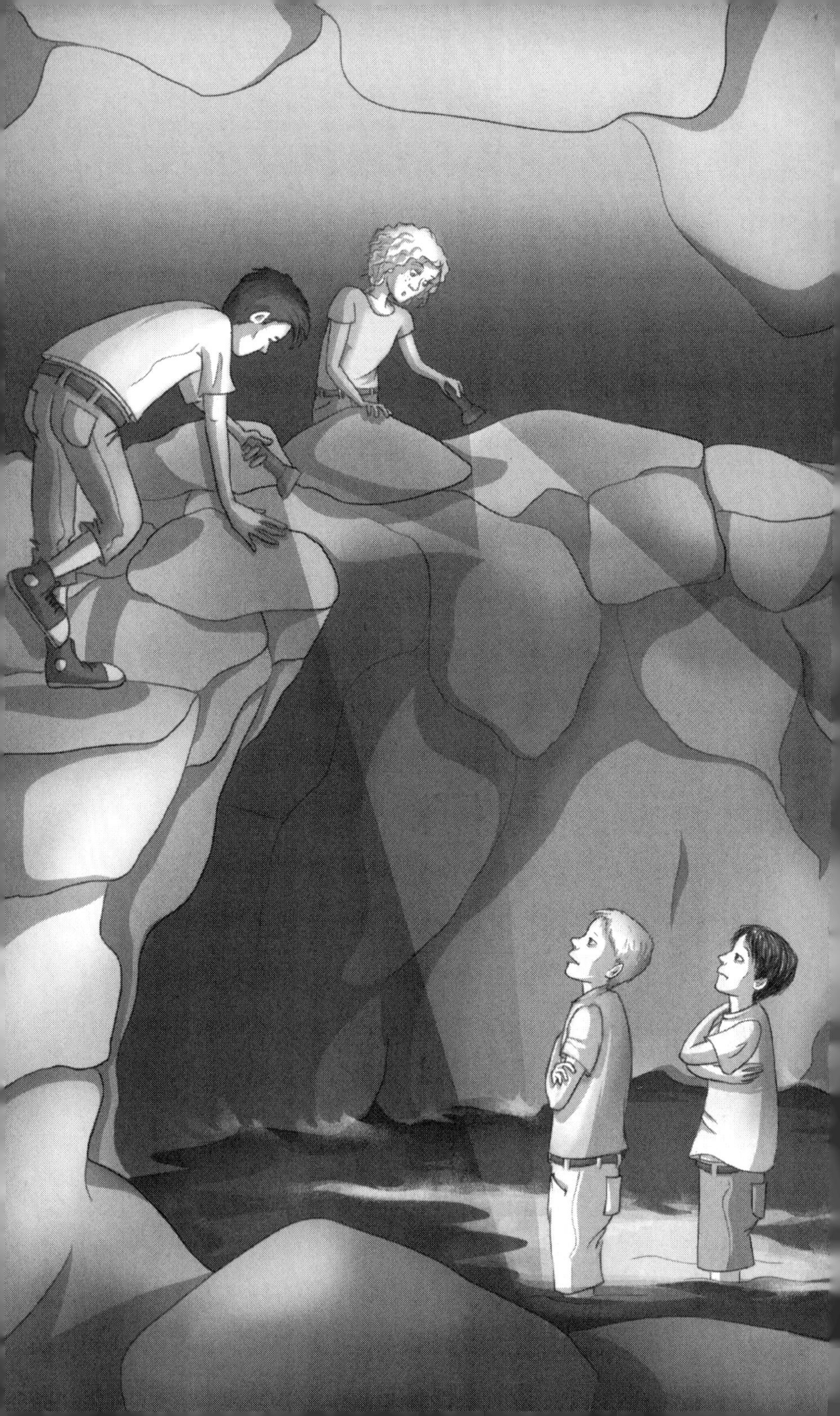

Chapter 18

A big surprise!

After a few, very long, hours, they began to hear the sea closer to their ears and realized it was already entering the opening of the cave. They left their backpacks and towels and hurried over, flashlights in hand. They crossed the opening. The foam of a receding wave splashed their face. Gomes was gone.

They slid down the rocks with a thousand cares, trying not to slip. Taking advantage of the moment when the sea retreated after pouring water down the hole, they got closer and pointed the flashlights downwards to the two boys.

"Are you all right?" Tony asked anxiously. He noticed the water was up to their knees and they were shivering from cold and fear.

They blinked and turned away from the light. They had been in utter darkness for so long that light hurt their eyes.

"We are, considering. Is that wretched Gomes gone? It seems we've been here for ages! Jack's been our sole companion. We've heard him screaming outside. The poor thing must be scared to death because he can't get in. Still, it looks like he took his revenge: he attacked Gomes again!"

"I did, too! I threw a passing crab at him and hit him in the face. You won't believe how scared he was! He left and never came back! Chris lost his flashlight and mine broke when I fell down here," Daniel said. His voice was hoarse from shouting. "We thought you'd gone to ask for help."

At that moment, a wave broke through the cave, knocking Bea and Tony down. They clung to the rocks so the water wouldn't push them down the hole.

The crashing wave made Chris and Daniel fall to the ground and cough. They got up and looked up anxiously. They both heaved a sigh of relief when they saw their heads again.

"You better get out of here. It's too risky! If you're not careful, you'll end up keeping us company," Chris warned with a slightly muffled voice.

"We can't leave you there! Chris, try to throw the rope up here!" his cousin asked. Sensing another wave was approaching, he held on as best he could. "There's another one coming, Bea! Take cover!"

A wave entered the cave, crashing furiously on the rocks, and flowed quickly down the hole.

Chris untied the rope, which was still wrapped around his waist, and tried to throw it at his cousin.

"I can't, Tony! It's soaked and really heavy! There's nothing I can do."

"Try again!"

The sea broke through the opening once again, pushing Tony towards the entrance to the cave. He hung there, trying hard not to fall on top of the others, clinging to the rock with his fingers. Bea pulled him up, drenched, before another wave knocked him down.

"Go away before another wave comes!" Daniel shouted.

"Listen! I have an idea! That cave is above sea level,

otherwise it would always be full of water, so it may not be completely flooded. All you need is to stay afloat until you get up here, then try to climb out and head towards the entrance to the caves and you'll be safe and sound! We'll go to the cave where the Image is and get some help!" Tony shouted, dodging another wave.

"We'll leave you the towels, some food and a flashlight in the pebble cave. You guys hide until we get back! Good luck!" Bea wished, forcing a smile when she saw them nod. They were very pale.

They finally managed to reach the entrance to the caves. Only one of the flashlights was on, to save the other flashlight for the other two. They walked down the passages, shivering with cold. After what seemed to them like hours, they got to the cave with the clustered pebbles. They wrapped themselves in a towel and leaned against each other to keep warm.

"They're gonna make it, Bea. You'll see! They are both tough!"

"I sure hope so! When we get warm, let's get out of here as soon as possible. Maybe we should have told them to hide in the other tunnel—the one we didn't explore. If those guys come looking for us, they won't catch all of us."

"Maybe Chris will think about that. Don't worry! You must be missing Jack a lot, too, aren't you?" Tony asked, sympathetically.

"I miss him so much! Things don't look so bad when he's around. I hope he's fine!" she said with a faint smile.

"I'm sure he is! Smart as he is!"

After some time, they had gathered enough courage to take the path that would lead them to the Chapel of Memory. They had a snack as fast as they could; they hadn't had anything yet that morning. They set out, feeling more comforted after they had rested and eaten. They tried not to think about what the brothers must be going through, but they couldn't push the thought away.

They remained silent all the way, walking more slowly, since there was only one flashlight. They got to the cave where the huge hole where Bea had fallen was and went round, cautiously. Shortly thereafter, they passed the chamber before the one where the Image was and then they were finally there. They crouched down, approaching the entrance.

Tony pointed his flashlight out but saw no one. Everything was in complete silence. Only a little light came through the small window opposite the Image.

"It must be dark outside. There's almost no light at all. Maybe it's drizzling," Bea said, looking at her cousin.

"We have to wait until someone shows up. That's weird! This place is always packed, especially in the summer! You may be right. It must be raining."

They sat on the ground and waited patiently. Finally, they seemed to hear some noise up. They listened. Someone was coming down the steps. They approached their faces to the bars, anxious.

An old lady dressed in black crossed herself before the Image and began to pray quietly, very concentrated.

"Pssst! Pssst!"

She was petrified. She stopped praying. Her eyes almost popped out of their sockets as she looked around. It seemed to her the noise had come from the Image.

"Pssst! Down here!"

She looked down and was terrified when she saw two very dirty faces, whose teeth and eyes glowed in a strange way. Her hair stood on end.

She yelled *"Our Lady of Nazareth, help me!"* and ran away. She slipped on the steps and crawled, scared to death. She closed the door behind her, as if she wanted to imprison those two strange creatures, which (needless to say) were the work of the devil, there.

Tony and Bea couldn't help laughing. Then they looked at each other, undecided.

"Maybe we should think of another plan."

"Wouldn't it be great if we could attract Gomes so that he would fall into that huge hole?" Bea suggested, her eyes shining. "It would be even better if he broke a leg!"

He laughed, shaking his head.

"Yeah, it would. If we do everything right, I'm sure we'll get him to fall into our trap. He's bound to come back when the tide is out. If he doesn't see us at the entrance, he'll have to come inside, at least to make sure we haven't escaped."

"We'll wait for him on the other side of the hole. When he sees us, we'll pretend we'll run this way and lure him into the hole."

They started their way back and sat patiently near the hole. With all those rocks and shadows, it would be extremely difficult for Gomes to notice it, just as it had happened to Bea when she fell inside.

They entertained themselves as best they could by chatting until Bea motioned her cousin to shut up. She seemed to have heard a noise. They remained silent, realizing that someone was heading there. Besides the footsteps, they heard mumbling.

They looked at each other, wondering whether it was the brothers or the enemy. They looked closely at the way out, silent as mice.

"Damn kids! Where did they go?" muttered a familiar voice. He pointed a powerful flashlight ahead and immediately found Bea and Tony, who pretended to be frightened."Ah! There you are!"

They got up and ran towards the steps. Gomes went after them, shouting at them to stop in an angry voice.

Somehow, he felt himself falling into space, dropping his flashlight.

He bumped down and landed on top of the skeletons. He checked the ground around him. He was sore.

"What the hell is this?!" he shouted, taking what appeared to be a large stone from under his bottom. When he saw a skull, lit by the children's flashlight, he almost jumped up and threw it to the ground, cowering in a corner. "Skeletons!"

They laughed mockingly.

"Looks like you're in good company, Mr. Gomes!" the boy said, pointing the flashlight to his eyes, forcing him to shield them.

"Give me a hand, will you, boy?"

"Like you gave my brother and my cousin? No, thanks! We like having you down there!"

"My partner will be here soon. You'll be in trouble then!"

"That's our problem. Maybe your little friend will also fall down that hole and you can keep each other company!"

"He won't fall. I'll let him know! You can't stop me from screaming!"

"That remains to be seen!" Bea said, in a threatening tone. She reached into the backpack and unexpectedly threw a pack of juice at his head, hitting the target. "That one's for my brother!"

Gomes raised his hand to his forehead, stunned. There was blood. He gave her a hateful gaze and threatened her with his other hand, clenched and bearing Daniel's teeth marks.

"You evil brat! Wait till I catch you!"

Another pack hit him in the nose. He groaned in pain. Tony laughed and Bea looked furious. When she was looking for another pack to throw at him, his cousin took her hand, stopping her.

"That's enough. We may need the others."

"That one's for Daniel, you treacherous scum!"

Gomes ground his teeth and said nothing else, afraid she might continue to attack him so ruthlessly. Deep down, he hoped she wouldn't start throwing stones at him. With her aim, God only knows what might happen to him!

"We should leave before that idiot's partner comes. Come on, Bea! We must move fast!" her cousin said, pushing her forward.

She looked at him questioningly. "Aren't we going to look for the others?"

"There's no time. The best way to help them is to get help as soon as possible. Besides, we don't know if they have already made it. We'd waste precious time looking for them."

Bea agreed and followed him, walking quickly.

They had been roaming those caves for so long now they felt they could do it with their eyes closed.

Suddenly, Tony stopped before they reached the pebble cave. His cousin bumped into him.

"Why did you stop?"

"Shhh. I think someone's coming!"

The little girl shuddered. Just when everything seemed to be going well! They remained silent. They hardly dared breathe. Whoever was coming from the other side had also stopped.

"Hold on," Tony whispered in Bea's ear.

"I can't hear anything."

They stood still for a while. They couldn't hear anything, so they started walking again. They immediately realized someone else had also started walking again. This time they seemed to hear two voices. They silently retraced their steps back to the cave where Gomes was and hid, turning off their flashlight.

The voices and footsteps were getting closer and closer. Suddenly, two beams of light swept across the cave. They crouched down as hard as they could, trying to go unnoticed. They couldn't see who was holding the flashlights, but they suspected who it might be.

"Tony... Chris... Are you there?" a voice they knew well asked.

They jumped up and pointed the flashlight to the newcomers.

"Godmom!"

"Zaza! I'm so glad it's you! We were afraid it was Gomes's friend!" the boy exclaimed, excited.

Suddenly, they were both speechless.

"What's he doing here with you, Godmom?" Bea asked. She couldn't believe her eyes.

Abel Cruz was the other person!

To their amazement, their godmother and that disgusting man embraced happily, as if they were good friends. They seemed crazy, patting each other on the back.

"We found them!"

The man looked at them mockingly. He burst out laughing, much to their amazement.

"Some detectives you are! You can't even recognize your Father."

The fake Abel Cruz straightened up. He was taller now. Slowly, he removed his false teeth, eyebrows, beard, and nose. He looked quite different from the weird guy they hated.

"Dad?! But... but..." the little girl stammered, running towards him and hugging him, almost crying, relieved. Now her father was there, she was sure everything would end well.

Tony smiled, delighted. His eyes shone like stars. He was so overwhelmed by emotion he couldn't speak.

"Where are the others?" their godmother asked, looking around her.

"We're not sure. We hope they got away and are hiding somewhere."

They heard someone moaning near them. The adults looked surprised. Bea smiled maliciously.

"That's Gomes. We threw him down that hole. Looks like he won't be going anywhere soon!"

"Leave him there. Now let's look for the others and get you all to a safe place. These people you messed with are very dangerous!"

"You don't say!" a voice behind them exclaimed. "For your sake, I hope you brought the CD."

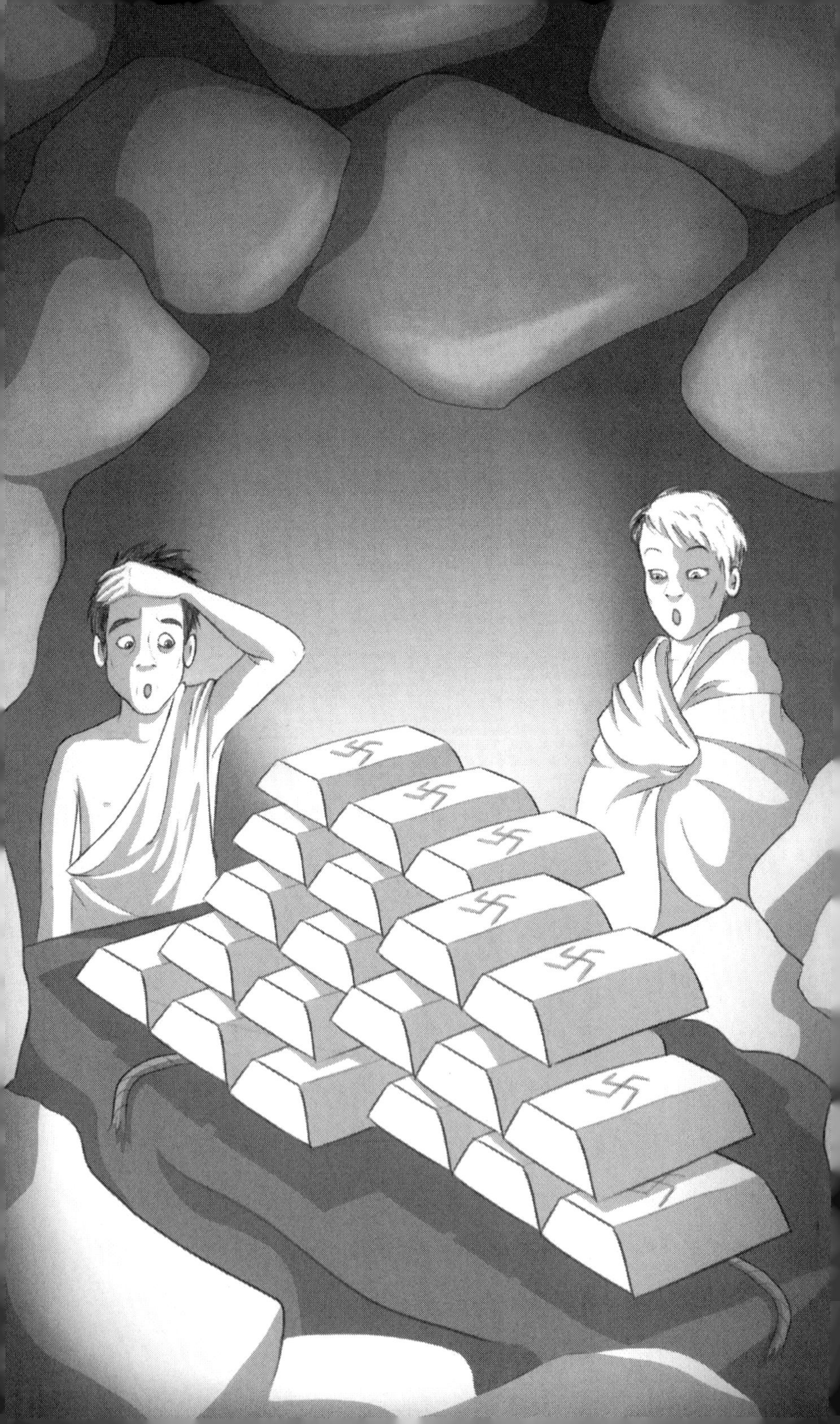

Chapter 19

An amazing discovery!

Meanwhile, what had happened to the other two boys since the moment Bea and Tony had left them? They had been in the dark again. They remained silent for a few minutes.

"Your brother's plan won't work, Daniel. I won't be able to stay afloat. I just can't!"

"Of course you can!"

"You don't understand, Daniel. I can't swim. I'm terrified of the sea. That's why I never want to go to the beach!"

His cousin stared at him and gasped. They had been leaning against one of the walls of the cave, so that the water would not hurl them to the ground again.

"I'll help you, Chris. We'll get out of here, you'll see!"

Chris looked at him, grateful he had not mocked his fear of the sea. They remained silent watching the cave fill with water little by little. It was already on their chest and kept going up and up until only their heads stood out. Their eyes had become accustomed to the darkness. They could see the opening through which the water ran.

Daniel swam towards it, dragging his cousin, who was almost paralyzed by fear. White foam splashed over their faces, making it hard for them to see. They waited for a wave to come and fall down the cave and then tried to reach the ledge quickly, which was a very difficult task, as everything was slippery.

Finally, Chris managed to hoist himself out as the sea reentered the cave. He nearly fell back down the hole again. He looked anxiously inside, trying to see his cousin, but there was no sign of him. The wave was powerful: he must have been submerged and was too tired to swim after helping his cousin for so long.

"Daniel! DANIEL!"

He feared the water less than he did not seeing his cousin ever again. He threw himself back into the hole, trying to find him.

He had some trouble finding him. He pushed him up so he could breathe. The two boys floated, panting. They hoisted themselves up, helping each other, even as a wave came crashing in again, leaving them breathless.

Chris dragged his cousin, realizing where the opening might be. They tumbled inside, plunged into complete darkness. They walked on all fours, shivering with cold. They were soaked to the bone and their teeth chattered.

It seemed to them that they had been walking along those subterranean spaces for hours until they reached the pebble cave. Walking in complete darkness feeling cold was not very pleasant. Fortunately, they had each other's company.

"Is it still a long way, Chris? I can't stand this much longer!"

"We must be close. Hey! I think this is it!"

They groped the ground. Chris gave an exclamation of joy. He had found the towels and the backpack. He sat on the ground and reached inside. He found what he was looking for. He switched on the flashlight, illuminating his cousin's face.

"Take off your wet clothes and wrap yourself in that towel, Daniel! We've been in the water for a long time. We must get warm!"

They took off their clothes and their shoes, rubbed themselves on the towels, and wrapped themselves around them. They looked rather comical. They opened the backpack and started to eat. They were starving. In the end, there were only half a dozen toffees left. They leaned against each other, feeling more comforted.

"I wonder if they managed to get out through the chapel cave," Daniel said, wringing his soaked sneakers as best he could.

"I hope so! We should hide anyway. That good-for-nothing Gomes may be back before help arrives. Let's explore the other tunnel. We'll be on the lookout for any possible noise that may warn us someone's coming."

They put their shoes on and started out. They felt their wet feet splashing inside their sneakers. Still, it was better than going barefoot: they might get hurt on the rocks.

They got to the cave and went through the other passage. They walked carefully, afraid there might be a hole.

"Watch out, Daniel! There are some steps here. They seem to be in a pretty bad shape!" Chris warned, stepping carefully.

They went down four steps carved in the rock and ended up in a small, low-ceilinged cave.

They crossed it and went into another cave. It was a little bigger and, to their great surprise, very bright.

"There must be a way out, Chris! Don't you think? There has to be!" Daniel exclaimed excitedly.

They continued to walk and found themselves in a much smaller cave than the previous ones. There was an opening facing the south side, as if it were a window. They saw the sky and moved closer, excited.

They immediately realized there was no chance of getting out through it. The opening was on the cliff wall! They could see the beach and the sea down below. There was no one there because of the fog that wetted their faces. They saw the strange shape of the frog carved in the rocks on the left. They went inside, discouraged.

"Just our luck! There's no way out here!" Chris said, saddened.

"It stinks! Seagulls must take shelter here, sometimes."

"I'd rather go back to the other cave. I can't stand looking outside knowing I can't get out."

His cousin agreed. They went back and sat on the floor together, leaning against the rock.

"I'll turn off the flashlight. We may need it later to find our way back. We can't risk running out of light just when we need it most."

And so they did. They slept a bit, though they kept waking up. Daniel shifted, uncomfortable. His behind was numb and cold. He started looking around after his eyes had become accustomed to the darkness. He noticed the strange wall that stood before them. It was much like the one at Forno d'Orca: there were long holes that looked like shelves. It seemed there was something inside. He shook his cousin.

"What is it? Is it time to go?" Chris asked, rubbing his eyes.

He switched on the flashlight and looked at his watch.

"It stopped!"

"Mine too. I don't know what time it is. I woke you up because of that!"

Chris pointed the flashlight to where his cousin was pointing at. He, too, was surprised. He stood up, curious.

"There seem to be several packages wrapped in black tarpaulin. How did they get here? How strange!"

They approached and touched the ropes binding the packages. Much to their surprise, they fell apart in their hands.

"How long has this been here? The sea air must have damaged the ropes," Chris said.

He threw the ropes to the floor and pushed aside the tarpaulin with the help of his cousin. What they saw left them breathless.

"Gold! So much gold! How cool is that?" Daniel said, rubbing his eyes as if he couldn't believe what they were seeing. "How did it end up here?"

He took a gold bar. It was very heavy! He couldn't look away.

"Nazi gold bars! Dozens of them! Can you believe what we found? We must be dreaming!"

The boys had a reason to be ecstatic. There were lots of shiny gold bars piled on top of each other. A swastika was engraved on each one.

They sat before that amazing find, pinching themselves to make sure they weren't dreaming. It was a strange feeling to have all that gold at your feet and within reach.

"It would probably take just one of them to solve all my parents' problems. They'd be able to pay the mortgage and maybe there would still be money left to buy new bikes," Daniel said, staring at a gold bar, his eyes shining.

Chris laughed. "You can't keep it, Daniel. Chances are it was stolen from the Jews during the Second World War and then melted and turned into gold bars. I just don't understand how it got here!"

They stopped for a few moments to observe that fantastic fortune and then went on to the next cave, the one with the opening on the cliff. It was dark outside. The foghorn from the lighthouse could be heard.

"It's dark already. We should go and see if we can get out. We have to be very careful. Gomes and Cruz may be around. Come on, Daniel! Bring the backpack! We must hurry! What are you doing? Let's go!"

Daniel ran after him. A few minutes later they heard a voice near them. They were startled.

«Rascal! Naughty boy! Dirty stinking scum!» a voice complained.

"Jack! We missed your nonsense so much!" Daniel exclaimed happily. "Come here, you naughty boy!"

As Chris pointed the flashlight around in search of the crow, Jack landed on his shoulder, pulling his hair softly. He was just as pleased to see them as they were. They patted him for a while.

The boy suddenly froze.

"Daniel, I think I saw light ahead. Did you see it, too?"

"I think so. Can it be Gomes?"

"What if it isn't? It could be someone looking for us. Let's follow it quietly and find out."

They continued to walk. Chris kept pointing the light of the flashlight to the ground, hoping whoever was walking ahead of them wouldn't notice it. They tiptoed as they came closer. The crow was as quiet as a mouse. He knew when he should be silent.

They stopped, stuck to the wall, flashlight off. A man was standing with his back to them a few feet ahead. They didn't recognize his voice, but, as his flashlight pointed ahead, they recognized Bea and Tony and the adults.

"Is that Godmom? How did she find out we were here? Who's that man? He's dressed like stupid Abel Cruz, but he looks different," Daniel whispered in his cousin's ear.

A smile lit up the other boy.

"It's Dad! Zazabeth managed to bring Dad! She understood my warning!"

"What warning?"

"I'll tell you about it later. We must understand what's going on. If that's what I think it is, we have to be quick. When I give you the signal, we'll get close quietly and hurl ourselves at the guy holding the flashlight!"

Daniel nodded, forgetting his cousin couldn't see him. He nudged him impatiently.

"Do you understand? You hit him in the legs. When he bends down, I'll hit him in the head. Then it's Dad's turn to act."

"I do, yeah. You can count on me. I can hit him if you want. I have the sort of thing right here," he replied with a wry smile.

Chris checked what he was holding and smiled. His cousin was the worst!

"Better not, Daniel. You might kill him."

"I must say I wasn't expecting to find you here. What a surprise to find out that the aloof Michael Soares was also the boring Abel Cruz. You really fooled us! It's a pity you won't live long enough to enjoy it," the other lodger of the house next door, which the children liked so much, said. His voice had lost its nice, charming tone. "Now, give me the CD, swiftly and carefully. You see, my little friend's a bit nervous."

Bea and Chris's Dad clenched his fists, furious. If he wasn't holding a gun, he would kick him hard. Then he noticed a strange movement behind his enemy and realized out of the corner of his eye that the others had also noticed.

"At least, let the kids go. They have nothing to do with this!" he said, trying to buy time.

Cruz, who the children knew as Jack Pereira, laughed.

"And lose the pleasure of taking revenge on what they and that damned crow did to me and my partner? You must be kidding! That evil bird lured me here, mimicking Nunes's voice, then it gifted me with all kinds of sneezes, coughs, sighs, and growls, which would put the bravest man's hair stand on end, only to discover it had been having fun at my expense all along! Still, it ended up doing me a great service! If I had not got inside looking for my partner, you'd be long gone by now and I'd be left standing here like an idiot. I just don't understand how that stupid crow knew my name is Jack."

«Nonsense, you fool! Nonsense!» Jack said. He couldn't be quiet anymore. Besides, his name had just been mentioned.

Cruz was astonished. It was as if he had heard himself saying those words.

Suddenly, before he had time to think, someone hit him on the legs with a hard object. He fell on his knees and was knocked over by someone who punched him again and again. Then the crow landed on him and pecked him until he begged for mercy.

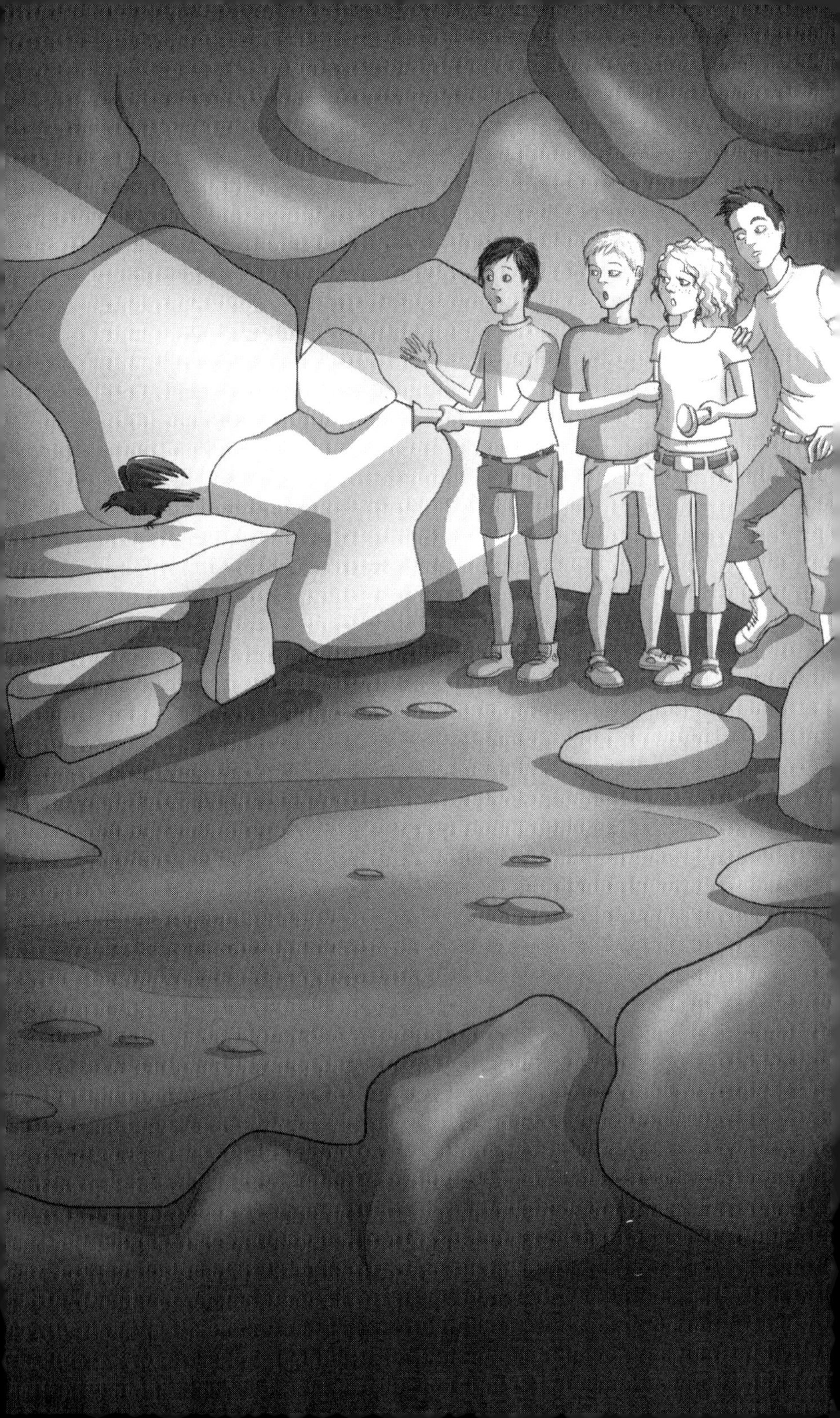

Chapter 20

Hell's Mouth!

Michael grabbed the gun and the flashlight at once. He nearly dragged Chris and Daniel away from Cruz. They seemed to have bet who would hit him the most. Apparently, it was a tie.

The others watched the scene in a lively mood. At last, it looked like everything was going to end well. They couldn't help laughing watching how ridiculous the two boys looked. They seemed to be in disguise, with those towels around their shoulders and their dirty faces.

"What did you hit him with, Daniel?" Bea asked, curious, pulling him close to her. Her eyes widened in astonishment when she saw what it was.

"You'll never guess what we found!" Daniel exclaimed.

The others gathered near him, ecstatic.

"You can tell us all about it later. We must deal with this wicked man first. Shall we throw him down the hole, too? They'd probably enjoy each other's company, don't you think?" Michael asked mockingly, as he put the gun to his back to force him to walk ahead of him. Everyone agreed, so he just pushed him down.

Cruz fell on top of Gomes, to his amazement. Gomes had not understood much of what had happened. They both grumbled in the dark.

"Soares! You're not going to leave us here in the dark with no food, are you?"

"Of course I am! It won't hurt you if you don't eat for a day or two. Also, we need the flashlights. I'm doing you a favor. You'd be bored to death if you had to stare at each other's mugs all the time!"

The other five laughed, amused. Jack flew off to the edge of the hole and began to walk to and fro.

«Nonsense, you fool! Rascal! Dirty stinking scum! Well, whaddya know?» he said, bursting out laughing at the men's anger.

Michael Soares put his hands on his son and his nephew's shoulders. They sat on the steps.

"Now, please tell me everything that happened to you. You'd better let Daniel and Chris speak first. They'll burst if they don't!"

The two boys told them their adventure in such an enticing way they were all excited.

"Nazi gold bars? How strange! How did they end up here?" Michael was puzzled.

Bea jumped up, moved.

"I know what happened! Michael, do you remember a German submarine appeared south of Pedra do Guilhim a few days after the end of World War Two? Dad told me about it once. He was a teenager back then, but he remembers seeing the submarine. The Coastal Patrol approached it and the German commander told them he wished to hand the submarine over to the authorities, as they had lost the war."

He smiled. It was all coming back to him now.

"Of course. I heard about it, too, but I'm not sure what happened."

"Oh, I do! The Germans landed in lifeboats and sat on the beach together. Then, unexpectedly, the submarine went down! The Germans had opened the valves, or whatever it is they're called, so that she would sink instead of ending up in the hands of the Allies! Dad remembers they did the Nazi salute as she sank!"

The four opened their eyes wide, excited. They seemed to be watching the scene unravel: the submarine going down and the Germans in uniform standing up and raising their arms towards the sea.

"A big fight had broken out. It seems that part of the crew wanted to go down with the submarine, whereas the other would rather surrender to the Allies to save their lives. As far as I know, one of them was even seen at the hospital in Sítio," Zaza said, her eyes shining. "Dad says that the ship's sonar beeps whenever he sails over the place where the submarine sank! Isn't this story great? I must write about it! It makes my entire body tingle!"

The others laughed. They knew what she meant.

"What happened to them?" Bea asked anxiously.

"They were taken to the Peniche Fortress. There were big fights among the prisoners, with stab wounds and all," Michael recalled. "Then they were sent to Lisbon to be handed over to the Allies."

"Yeah. The word on the street was that there were English prisoners in the submarine and that the Nazis had sunk her so as not to hand them over," their godmother added, smiling at the children.

"If the submarine sank, then how did the gold end up here, Zaza?" Tony asked. He, too, found that story exciting.

"Do you know what I think? The Nazis must have checked Praia do Norte first. As there was no one on the beach, some of them must have landed in the lifeboats and hid the gold so they could retrieve it one day after they were released. They must have found the entrance to the caves by chance and thought it was a good hiding place," she said. She seemed to be daydreaming.

"Then why didn't they come?"

"Perhaps the few people who knew about it died in the Fortress during the fights or somewhere else and the secret of the gold's fate was lost forever. How extraordinary that it was you who found it!" she said, giggling. "I won't leave this place without having a look at it, Michael! I'll die if I don't!"

He hugged her, laughing out loud.

"Let's go then! You go ahead with the boys. After all, it was you who started the whole thing."

«Let's go then! Well, whaddya know? Nonsense!»

They got on the way, so overwhelmed by joy they felt like jumping up and down and screaming. As always, Jack was on his owner's shoulder, sneezing.

They got to the treasure cave shortly afterwards. They stood there admiring all that gold for a moment. They touched it, almost breathless.

"I wonder if I could keep one of these. They're so cool! And they would make my parents smile!" Daniel said hopefully.

"I don't think so, Daniel. This gold doesn't belong to us. It must be handed over to the government, which in turn will be in charge with finding its rightful owners," Michael replied, patting him on the shoulder. "Which doesn't mean you won't receive a reward for what you've done. The police, at least, will certainly be grateful to you for having prevented that CD from falling into the hands of those two unscrupulous rascals."

"What's so special about the CD anyway, Uncle?" Tony asked, dying of curiosity.

"A very important list of names. That's all I can tell you, as you must understand!"

They nodded.

"Now, move! I'm starving!"

They resumed their journey. When they were close to the way out of the caves, they suddenly bumped against each other.

"What's up, Uncle?"

"Shhhhh! I can hear voices."

They shivered, worried. They hadn't seen that coming. They thought they were safe. Now it seemed they weren't going to see the light of day anytime soon. They remained silent. They heard several voices speaking at the same time. Interestingly, you could barely hear the waves.

"Go back and wait for me in the pebble cave. I'll try to find out who it is."

They obeyed him, upset.

Michael peered at the entrance to the cave and stepped back. The shadow of two people had blocked the light entering the cave. He frowned, annoyed, then went back to meet the others. They were sitting, as quiet as mice.

"So, Michael?"

"We can't leave. There are at least two at the entrance."

They looked at each other, concerned.

"All we can do is try to go out through the Chapel of Memory."

"We can try, but it'll be extremely difficult to get out through there. It's worth a try, though."

"Well, the best we can do is eat something and get on our way."

Everyone agreed. They sat down and ate the cheese sandwiches Michael had brought.

Suddenly, Bea realized Jack wasn't there. She stood, worried.

"What's up, Bea?"

"Jack's not here. Where did that crazy bird go? Do you think he went back to the caves?"

"Maybe he wanted to scare those two crooks," Daniel said.

"If that's the case, I feel sorry for them. It mustn't be pleasant to sit in a hole in the dark, unable to get out, surrounded by skeletons and listening to strange moans and chilling coughs," Chris said with a smile.

The others smiled as they pictured the scene.

"They must be clinging to each other, shivering from fear," Michael joked, trying not to burst out laughing.

"Don't worry, Bea. He probably couldn't take it anymore and flew off outside. I can see his point," his godmother said.

"I'll check the entrance to the cave. Maybe I can hear him."

She left before anyone was able to stop her. She kept pointing her flashlight to her feet. She was afraid another partner of the two rascals might hurt her beloved crow out of revenge.

Bea reached the entrance to the cave and turned off her flashlight. She peeked. As she saw no one, she walked cautiously over the rocks, afraid she might slip. She listened carefully. She heard voices very close to her. They seemed to come from outside the cave. They must be the other men's friends waiting for their return, guarding the entrance so they wouldn't be able to leave.

She frowned. She had expected to hear Jack messing with them, but she didn't. The crow had not flown off to the beach.

Suddenly, she heard a muffled cough. Interestingly, it seemed to come from the ground. She ducked down by the hole and pointed the flashlight downwards.

Jack was hopping on the ground of the small cave where the boys had been a few hours earlier, shaking off the sand that clung to his paws.

"Jack, you idiot! Come! Let's go!"

Jack let out a squeak, sulking. He knew he shouldn't have flown off like that, but he couldn't take it anymore. As he was about to go outside, something very bright caught his attention. It came from the bottom of the cave. He couldn't fight his curiosity, so he flew down there to check what it was.

It turns out he had been drawn by the flashlight from one of the boys, which was lying there. He was very disappointed!

Bea laid flat on the ground and stretched out her arm so that he could land on it, but Jack had different plans. He was still hopping around. He seemed to have forgotten how to fly.

"Come here, Jack! Hurry up! Those men may return any minute! Come, you fool! I feel like flicking you so much for disobeying me right now!" the little girl exclaimed, unnerved. Even though she stretched even more, he didn't obey her, either because he was afraid of being punished or for some other reason.

Somehow, Bea lost her balance and crashed on the ground. She sat up, feeling a little stunned.

Jack flew to her shoulder, muttering something in a plaintive tone. He didn't like that hole in the ground at all.

"I fell because of you, you rascal! Now I really should hit you!"

The crow pecked her ear tenderly. She patted him.

"You're such a naughty boy! Poor Jack! You must be tired of being inside these caves!"

«Poor Jack! Naughty boy!»

"That's right! You're a naughty boy! Now, let's try to find my flashlight. I hope it didn't break when it fell!"

She felt the ground and found it after searching for a while. Fortunately, it still worked. She pointed it to the ceiling.

"Now I'll have to wait for the others to help me out. Dad won't be happy I got into trouble because of you. Anyway, since I'm here, I might as well take a look at that hole we saw the other time."

She came close and pointed her flashlight to the round hole.

"You can crouch your way in. Where will it lead to? I wish I could explore it! If I just take a look and return in no time, Dad will never know."

She went through the hole, unfortunately for Jack, who was fed up with so many holes and caves. All he wanted was to fly off to the beach and see the sunlight.

"Jack, come here!"

He didn't budge.

Bea crouched. She was so excited her heart seemed to leap in her breast. She stopped now and then, pointing the flashlight ahead of her. She was delighted, picturing their faces as she told them she had already explored the opening they had seen.

The small tunnel was level for a few feet. Suddenly it went downwards so much she slipped and tumbled down. Though she kept trying to hold on to something, the slime on the walls made it terribly slippery.

After a few seconds that seemed like minutes, Bea landed on something soft. She checked what it was with her hand: sand. At least she didn't land on a rock - she might be hurt then. She sat up, sore. Much to her annoyance, she had lost her flashlight. Her eyes could only see darkness all around her.

She felt a chill run through her entire body. Where was she? Did she end up in a cave under the sea? There was nothing she could do without a flashlight. She couldn't see a thing. She couldn't walk in the dark and risk falling into a hole.

She could hear the incessant roar of the sea down there, which made her feel many different things. She regretted not having waited for the others. She just wished they would come to her aid quite soon.

They had waited for her for a while. As she didn't return, they set out, afraid she might have been caught by one of Gomes's men.

"You may come. I can't see anyone at the entrance to the cave."

They came down the rocks carefully. Daniel peered down at the beach.

"They're still there, Uncle. I saw two men talking right below. That's funny! The opening seemed to be closer to the sand before."

"I wonder where Bea is," Tony murmured, worried.

They heard a plaintive voice.

«Poor Jack! Poor Jack! Naughty boy!»

"Dad! He's down there!" Chris shouted, astonished. He had forgotten he should speak softly.

"If Jack is there, she can't be far away. BEA! BEA!"

Michael produced a rope he was wearing around his waist and tied it firmly to a solid-looking rock.

"You go! I'll be on the lookout. Hurry up!" he said, sitting down as comfortable as he could.

They went down the rope one by one, holding their flashlights tight. They got to the small cave sometime later. Jack landed on Daniel's shoulder, happy to see them again after being alone for so long.

"Michael, Bea's not here! I wouldn't be surprised if she had decided to explore that opening," their godmother said. "I'll stay here while they explore the hole. They may need help. Daniel, grab Jack and don't let him fly off again!"

Tony got in through the opening, followed by Daniel and Chris, who would rather have stayed in the cave. Still, his sister was in distress. He understood how worried his father was, even though he didn't show it so as not to upset them.

"Bea! BEA!"

They heard a muffled voice.

"I can't make out what Bea is saying. Be careful not to slip, guys! It'll probably get slippery any moment now. This place must be full of water when the tide goes up. I think we're going DOOOOOWWWNN!"

Just like Bea, they came tumbling down the tunnel. They landed on top of the amazed girl, knocking her over and scaring her to death.

"Get your knee out of my mouth!"

"Who's sitting on my foot?"

"Rats! I'm all sore! You could have warned us, Bea!" Daniel said, checking his legs and arms for broken bones.

"I did warn you! You didn't understand what I said!"

Tony pointed his flashlight to her to make sure she was okay.

Daniel snatched the flashlight from his brother's hand. What he saw made him exclaim in amazement. Bea did the same to her brother, pointing the flashlight in the same direction.

The four gaped, astonished.

A table and two benches crudely carved in the rock stood before them.

They could hardly believe their eyes. They were standing before the table and the benches their great-grandmother had talked about. So it was true! They were in Boca do Inferno!

They were at a loss for words. Even Jack was speechless, as if he, too, was puzzled by the strange find.

They ran their fingers through the table and the benches and then sat down. They all had a very special feeling.

"Can you believe no one has sat here for ages? I wonder who he last ones to do it were," Bea said, excited.

"Maybe they were pirates!" Daniel replied at once.

The others laughed. Their laughter echoed through the strange cave. They shivered. Jack let out a startled squeak. He was even more startled when he heard his squeak echoing through the cave. He really didn't like those weird, smelly places the children insisted on roaming.

"Don't you find it very strange that this cave is not full of water? It should be!" Chris said, walking around, noticing barnacles clinging to the cave walls.

Tony agreed. He walked around the cave. It was large and round.

"Come here! Do you see this huge pile of sand at my feet? I bet this is the entrance to the cave!"

"Why is it covered then?"

"I don't know. Something strange happened. This can't be right. I wonder what it was."

"Come here! I found an opening! Maybe it's a way out!" Bea said.

They ran up to her and watched the narrow opening that went almost all the way to the ceiling.

"I'll go ahead. Wait here!" Tony said.

They refused to part with him. They went in next, one by one. Bea held on to Jack, realizing he was getting ready to fly away. They walked on level ground. Then the path went up all the way. It seemed to them it headed straight for the lighthouse.

They had some trouble walking. They skinned their legs on some sharp rocks, but they never gave up.

They walked for a few minutes that seemed endless to them. Suddenly, Tony let out a scream. They jumped up, frightened.

"What happened?"

"What is it? Spit it out!"

"You won't believe it! You just won't believe it!"

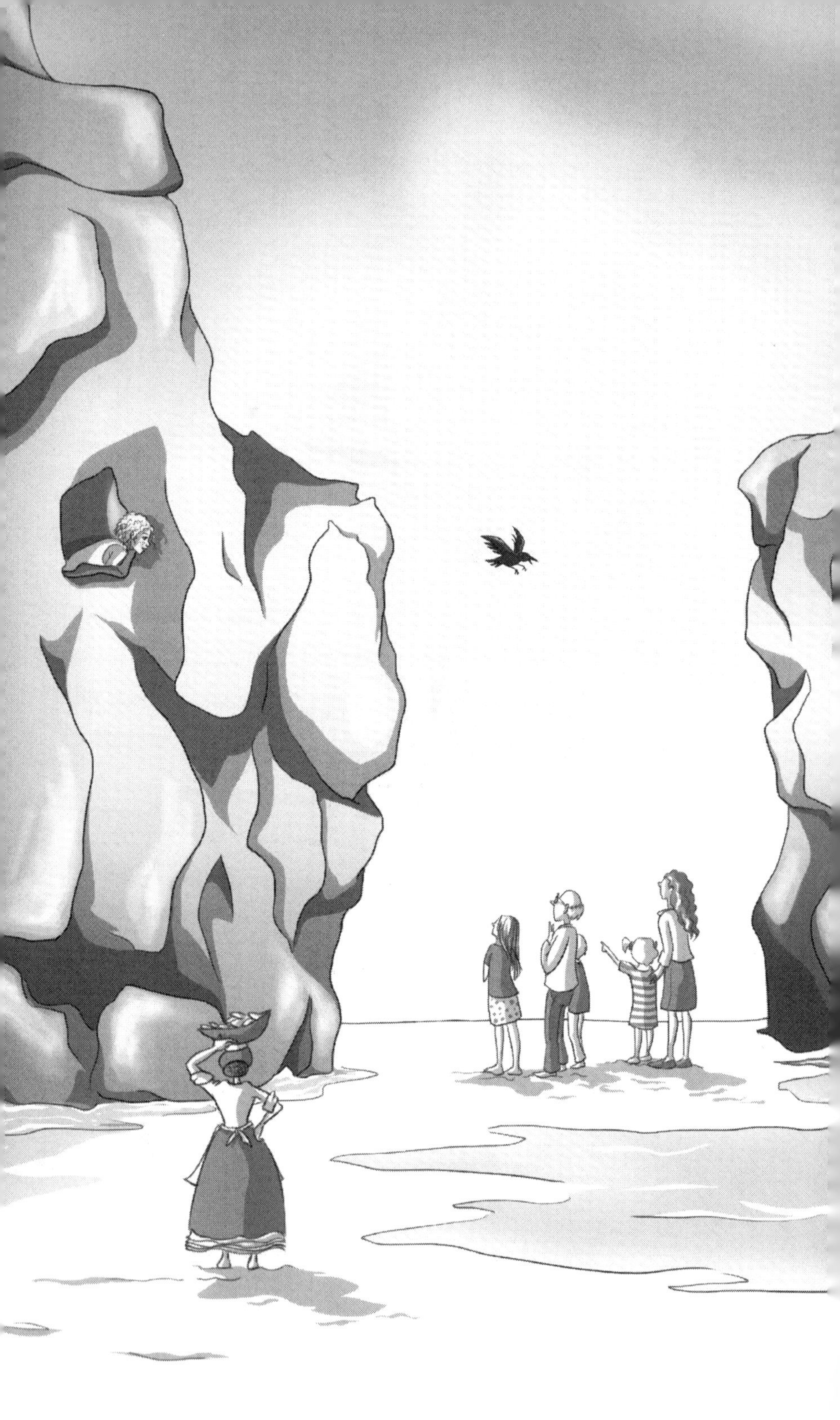

Chapter 21

A very happy ending!

"The sea retreated, forming a small beach right next to Pedra do Guilhim! There's tons of people here!"

"WHAT?!?"

"I don't buy it! You're making fun of us!" Bea said, incredulous.

"It's true! There's no sea between Pedra do Guilhim and the cliff where the lighthouse is! There's lots of people looking at me and laughing. They all look crazy! They're walking to and fro, embracing and greeting each other, happy as can be. There's even a tent here!"

"WHAT?!"

"Get out of there, Tony! I want to see it, too!" Daniel said, nervous.

"There's no need. I'm going to jump onto the sand."

To his friends' amazement, he jumped onto the ground, scaring a woman wearing traditional local clothes who was walking around looking respectfully at the cliff.

Bea's head appeared at the entrance to the opening. Her eyes widened in astonishment. Everything his cousin had said was true. There was no sea there. They could walk near the huge rock that the locals called Pedra do Guilhim, nobody knows why. They could even touch it if they wished. The others followed, each one more astonished than the other.

Jack flew off, laughing out loud and saying the usual nonsense, making everyone laugh. No one thought it was strange that they had come out of an opening in the cliff. No wonder: the sea had retreated on that spot, which had not happened in the past fifty years!

The children breathed in the air, amazed! They hadn't done it for so long! They were laughing and running around, sharing everyone's joy and enthusiasm. There were men on top and around Pedra do Guilhim, scraping off the barnacles that kindly clung to it. Others were doing the same on the cliff, in places that were usually under water.

"How did this happen?" Tony asked a fisherman he knew.

"It's a true phenomenon, my lad. The same thing happened when I was a boy like you. A huge pile of sand was deposited here by the tide. That's why you can walk through here now."

Suddenly, Chris burst out laughing. The other three were startled. Jack mimicked him. Everyone around was pleased.

"Do you know what I think? All those voices that we heard near the opening of the cave, which we thought were Gomes and Cruz's partners in crime, were just excited people exploring all the openings that are usually under the sea. That's why it seemed to Daniel that the cave was higher up than when we got in."

"That reminds me! We must warn Zaza and your Dad!"

"I'll go!" Daniel immediately said, disappearing from their sight.

He was back a few minutes later, accompanied by his godmother, who was looking around, delighted, and Michael, who was as excited as everyone else.

They told them the news, each one more enthusiastic than the others. The adults envied their luck. Who knew they would find Hell's Mouth! They would have liked to have followed them there, but the opening was too narrow for them.

It was a beautiful day. The fog was gone.

Michael knelt at the foot of the cliff and began to dig the sand. "From what you said, the opening must be in this direction. Have you ever thought how much sand the sea brought here to the point of covering it completely? What a phenomenon!"

They agreed. Their eyes were shining.

Jack tried to pronounce that new word but failed, which made him sad.

They stayed there for some time. Little by little, people were beginning to leave that place even though they did not want to. The tide was going up and the waves were breaking at the foot of the cliff.

They went around the cliff and came near the opening through which they had entered the underground caves. They'd never be able to do it on their own now: it was quite high up above. Next to it there was another round opening. They tried to explore it. The small tunnel, about twenty-six feet long, led to another opening below, which was usually covered by the sea.

"How come we didn't notice this opening? It's right next to the one we entered!" Bea said, amazed.

"It must have been covered by the sea," Chris replied, jumping onto the sand, and sitting down, tired.

"Come here! There's another opening here! It seems to go all the way to the lighthouse!" Daniel shouted, excited.

They ran towards him. There was a huge cave, full of openings. They climbed up with the help of the adults and peered through an opening.

"The opening leads to the lighthouse for sure, Zaza! You can see light up there! It goes up all the way. It's so steep it must be extremely difficult to climb."

"Can we explore it, Dad? Can we?" Bea asked, excited.

The other three immediately joined in. Their godmother laughed, amused. Jack gave a high-pitched laugh, surprising the people who were nearby.

Her father shook his head firmly.

"No, you can't. Leave it for some other time. We need to bring some special gear. It's very dangerous to go inside without ropes. Now, go! I still have to deal with the two rascals trapped in the cave."

"What a pity! We may not get another chance to do it!" Bea said, gazing at the ground.

"I wish the sea would remain like that for a long time!" Daniel said. They all agreed.

The two adults laughed at their sadness.

"There will be other chances. You must be tired after walking for hours on end! If I were you, I'd be out like a light and snoring like a bear by now!"

Everyone laughed.

They walked up to Forno d'Orca, talking about the places they had explored. The two adults looked at each other, proud of the courage the children had shown.

They were running out of gas by the time they reached the road. The four children looked longingly at the place where they had left their bikes. As they expected, they were long gone.

"Pop went our bikes!" Daniel complained, devastated. "I should have hit that treacherous rascal harder!"

The others laughed, even though they also felt very sorry for what had happened.

"Never mind. Perhaps you'll get a bicycle each as a reward for your courage!" Michael said, mysterious.

They looked at each other, hopeful. They got into the car and sat as best they could. Their godmother sat in the front seat. They looked back, longingly recalling everything they had gone through in the last few days.

It had been a wonderful adventure!

They arrived at Tony and Daniel's place sometime later. They were so tired they could hardly stand. They fell flat on their beds without taking their clothes off (they were much too tired for that!) and slept until dinnertime. Their parents had been brought up to date in the meantime. They could hardly believe all those adventures had happened to them without their knowledge. Christine shivered.

When they came down to dinner, they went straight to the kitchen and had a hearty meal. The dessert was an extremely appetizing huge yellow *Molotof* pudding, of course—there was little left afterwards. Then they joined the others, who were talking about the recent events in the living room.

To their great surprise, four identical (except for the color) brand new bicycles were there. They could hardly believe their eyes. They ran towards them, their eyes shining, and each chose their own, thanking heartily.

"That's your reward. As for the other two, they were taken by the police, and the gold has already been handed over to the authorities," Michael said, smiling broadly at their happy faces.

"Cool!" they exclaimed at the same time.

"You should have seen the look on your faces whenever you looked at me! It was a gas! It was so hard not to laugh!" Michael confessed, bursting out laughing. They all did the same—including Jack, of course.

"That was very naughty of you, Dad! Saying all that nonsense with such a poker face!" Bea said, sitting on his lap, laughing amusedly.

«Nonsense! Naughty boy! Nonsense, you fool! Wake up, lazy girl!» Jack said as he lovingly pulled her hair.

Michael patted his head, good-naturedly.

"Jack was smarter than all of you put together. He was the only one who recognized me. I even thought he had revealed my disguise when he started shouting *Wake up, lazy girl!*

whenever he was next to me. You must confess you weren't so smart in that department."

"Even Mom wouldn't recognize you in that disguise!" Chris commented, smiling, recalling the creature they all found disgusting.

"Well, someone found out. I must say I was a little careless, considering I was playing my part so well," Michael confessed, sad.

"I've got it! It was Godmom at Tony's birthday party! I remember seeing her looking at you, very amazed!" Bea recalled, turning to her godmother. "Why did you suspect him?"

Her godmother laughed out loud, amused.

"As always, your father couldn't resist sticking his finger and kneading the *Molotof* pudding with his fingers! When I saw him doing it and looking so satisfied, I immediately remembered I had seen him do the same many years ago, when I was younger than Daniel. Of course, when he saw me staring at him that way, he couldn't hide it from me any longer and I recognized him!"

The others laughed out loud.

"Shame on you, Uncle!" Daniel scolded him, waving his index finger right in front of his nose.

"I gave you some clues to suspect I wasn't what I seemed to be: I prevented Gomes from following you, don't you remember? You should have seen how mad he was! He was furious! I had so much fun with all the nasty things Jack did, too! The hardest thing was not washing my hair for a while. Everyone was so disgusted when they looked at it! Of course, I also shaved all the hair on the back of my hands to better disguise myself, otherwise it would have been a dead giveaway. I hadn't had that much fun in ages!"

"Why did you decide to disguise yourself, Uncle?" Tony asked, sitting on the arm of the sofa, leaning against his mother.

"I was worried you might be followed, so I wanted to be close in case you needed me. Of course, I couldn't let you recognize me: one of those rascals might be suspicious. I left your mother safely and came here as fast as I could. I was right. Still, I must admit choosing the surname Cruz was a big coincidence."

"Yeah. I heard that fake Gomes calling someone Cruz on the phone."

"Which was why we were convinced Abel Cruz was in it together with Gomes—I mean, Nunes!" Chris ended, with a smile.

"There's one thing I haven't quite figured out yet. How did you find out where we were, Godmom?"

She smiled, pleased.

"Chris called me Zaza in the letter he wrote to me. Tony's the one who does that; Chris always calls me Zazabeth. I realized he was drawing my attention to something in the letter without Gomes noticing. When he asked me to pray to my favorite saint, St Romano, I immediately deduced where they might be. I don't know any St Romano. The only Romano I know was Friar Romano. I came to your Father and we decided to look for you. We waited for the tide to go down and you already know the rest!"

The others looked at the boy, surprised. Chris blushed and smiled at Daniel, who hadn't told anyone what had happened between them. It was their secret. The two felt more united than ever. It was as if they'd always been friends.

"You know what? I've just remembered where I had seen Gomes before. He was in the train corridor on our way here! He was standing by the window and was nearly toppled by that little old lady who was fleeing her compartment because Jack here had been having fun at her expense!" Bea said, laughing amusedly—and being mimicked by her beloved Jack.

They all laughed, looking at the crow. Jack burst out laughing, which made them laugh even more. Then he mimicked a dry cough and finally ended with a monumental sneeze.

"It seems Jack had at least as much fun as you did! He kept pecking Gomes and Cruz! Those two were in a pitiful state. In addition to Daniel biting his hand, Gomes had a broken nose and a big bump on his forehead. It seems Miss Bea used him for target practice!" Michael said with a malicious look.

"I wouldn't like to have you as my enemies!" the boys' Father said, smiling. He was very proud of the way they had behaved against all odds. "You are brave adventurers indeed!"

"Looks like I was right after all, wasn't I, Sis? At the end of the day, they managed to overcome their differences and become friends. All it took was to find the right reason for them to come together."

"That's all very nice, but you could have found a much simpler and less dangerous reason. Still, you're right: they learned a lot from each other. I just hope they'll never argue again," Christine said, smiling at the children, satisfied that all had ended well. Even she found it hard to believe the dangers they'd been in.

"We still haven't found out where you hid the CD, Godmom," Daniel said, curious. The others surrounded her. They were curious, too.

"You'd never guess! I stored it in a file on my computer as a precaution. I made up a story and inserted it somewhere in the middle. I did my best to make it extremely boring, so no one would be interested in reading it," she informed them with a malicious laugh. "Then I wrapped the CD very carefully and hid it in a nest in the fig tree behind my place."

They looked at her in amazement. It would never occur to them to use it as a hiding place.

"Since we're all confessing stuff, I'd like to know who gave me the slice of pudding on the day I behaved very badly," Daniel said, looking at his mother, suspicious.

Bea smiled, amused. "I did. I felt I was also to blame. I didn't want you to go without the dessert you like so much."

Daniel smiled at her, pleased. He didn't understand how he had ever hated her so much. He liked her a lot now, even though he preferred Chris.

«Well, whaddya know? Nonsense, you fool! Nonsense! Well, whaddya know? Naughty boy!», Jack said, bursting out laughing, mimicking his owner's father, who had a very funny laugh.

"You're the naughty boy!" Bea replied, patting his beak. "But we wouldn't live without you, you crazy bird!"

«Crazy bird! Well, goodbye! See you never!»

Goodbye, Tony! Goodbye, Bea and Jack! Goodbye, Chris and Daniel! It was really nice meeting you. We hope to see you again very soon, on new adventures! After all, you are **THE ADVENTURERS!**

About the Author

ISABEL RICARDO wrote her first adventure book at 11 years old and has published several books in Portugal and abroad. Her fascinating writing has enamored readers of all ages. She loves to travel to places that serve as inspiration for her books, as well as speaking with students, in reading incentive sessions that are promoted by schools and libraries.

The closeness she keeps with her readers results in a bond which leads to a special friendship and a huge enthusiasm over her books. In addition to being a renowned author of children and youth literature, suggested by many Portuguese teachers, she also writes historical novels. She lives in Paço de Arcos, Lisbon.

Printed in Poland
by Amazon Fulfillment
Poland Sp. z o.o., Wrocław